GRAVITY DRIFT

A Journey to Europa

John Charles Miller

This book is an original publication of John Charles Miller.

ISBN: 9798343013382

Self-published by John Charles Miller

Cover by Rocking Book Covers …rockingbookcovers.com

Cover photos: NASA

ACKNOWLEDGMENTS

Thanks to my two helpful Beta Reviewers for getting this Space Murder/Mystery on the right track.

MaryAnn Sciavillo-Lopéz, Author of the Titanic-themed novel *Sail Again* and its follow-up, *The Gateway's Continuum.* And her bookstore ghost story, *Whispers in the Attic.*

Mary Lu Scholl, Author of Florida cozy, fun to read, mysteries without a lot of blood, sex, and violence. She writes a series: *Nature Coast Calamities.*

And to:

Mary Miller, My amazing wife of fifty-six years. The bluebird monitoring queen of Tampa, Florida, with a 56-box bluebird trail in Flatwoods Park. She made the final review... A voracious reader, she knows what is worthwhile reading or viewing. I am pleased with her efforts and much appreciative.

Adrijus Guscia of RockingBookCovers.com for working with me to prepare, as usual, an excellent cover.

NASA for online guidelines as to how to use photos and selected text from Europa Clipper project summaries.

PREFACE

Gravity Drift is intended to be a stand-alone novella. It can be read as such.

However, much of the background to the story-line is based on the four-book Florida Murder/Mystery series:

- **The Listener**
- **The Nose Knows**
- **Legging It**
- **Bloody Crocs**

Reading these four earlier books is not required for understanding Gravity Drift. However, reading them will enhance the understanding and development of the various characters and how Hera-Juno came to be on the Europa Inspector spacecraft.

JOHN CHARLES MILLER'S BOOKS

Citrus White Gold – Alternate History Novel of Citrus County, Florida. (Florida Time-Travel Series – Book One), 2012.

You Can't Pick Up Raindrops – a collection of short stories. 2012.

Dead Not Dead – a parallel universe romance novella. 2013.

He Hears The Rocks – a collection of short stories/poetry. 2015.

The Gatherers – A Sequel to Citrus White Gold. (Florida Time-Travel Series --- Book Two), 2017.

Deep Florida – A Sequel to Citrus White Gold and The Gatherers. (Florida Time-Travel Series --- Book Three), 2019.

Juice – The humorous story of Zombies in the Missouri Ozarks wanting to be "regular people" is a novella. 2020.

The Tale of the Black Umbrella – a romantic novelette. 2020.

The Listener – a Florida Murder/Mystery novel. (Missus Gurley and Milo Series), 2020.

The Nose Knows – a Florida Murder/Mystery novel. (Missus Gurley and Milo Series), 2021.

Legging It – a Florida Murder/Mystery novel. (Missus Gurley and Milo Series), 2021.

Bloody Crocs –A Florida Murder/Mystery novel. (Missus Gurley and Milo Series), 2022.

Wheels & Ruedas – a dual-language (English/Spanish) collection of short stories and novelettes. 2023.

Shifting Sands – a Florida Murder/Mystery Novel, 2023.

Gravity Drift – a space murder/mystery novella, 2024

CHAPTER ONE

Warning

Late 2034

Good Morning, Hera-Juno! It's a wonderful morning here with NASA at John F. Kennedy Space Center on Merritt Island, Florida, a bit of rain and slightly windy, but at least no hurricanes are forecasted. Not too early for one, of course. Always on the alert," Berks transmitted to the Europa Inspector* spacecraft.

"You, of course, are five times as far from the Sun as we are, so not as bright a day way out there near Europa. Only about 3.7 percent of the same light as on Earth. However, it's still morning. Time to wake up, sleepyhead!

"I'm here with old Eddie, looking over my shoulder. Sorry to interrupt your always busy schedule, but we need to talk. It's critical. Please look at the attached data."

Hera-Juno welcomed hearing from NASA, especially Berks's and Eddie's bantering humor. Although she was not alive as a human, she sometimes needed friendly contact.

She read the brief message, ignoring the attached files and supporting calculations, knowing what it was about, and showing no sign of concern on her part. She had no use for fear and didn't want NASA to assume otherwise. She had accepted her new life and the absolute, unescapable ending. It was something she could not change. However, it angered her.

Messages to and from Hera-Juno are delayed or are often fragmented due to the average 365 million miles between Earth and her "new home" in the Europa Inspector spacecraft. So, there is a pause between messages sent and responses. And, briefly, there is no communication when the moon Europa, which she orbits in elliptical flybys, is behind the gigantic planet Jupiter. However, at this time the spacecraft was well-positioned for reliable contact as the spacecraft had moved into a new elliptical orbit.

Depending on the position of Jupiter from Earth, the communication time between them ranges from a bit more than 35 to a bit less than 55 light minutes, using the speed of light, 186,00 miles per second. So, when they make contact, NASA knows that she's telling them about recent events and supplying new observational data, except for the impact of the time lag. Neither she nor the NASA staff mind this. There is always something interesting to exchange.

Rogers Berkshire and Edmund Faulke are flight control officers at NASA/KSC for the Europa Inspector spacecraft. They were the first to discover that Hera-Juno had covertly gotten through their closely monitored pre-launch programs and into the spacecraft's computer memory just before launch from KSC.

NASA's communication with Hera-Juno is in a compressed electronic form that she can "read". When she talks to them, they receive it as a text printout, decompressed.

Residing in the spacecraft's memory banks she says to herself, *As if I don't know what this is all about. I've been monitoring the situation as well.*

Responding, "And, good morning to you both. I suppose life in sunny Florida is the same as always, herds of obnoxious tourists and newcomers, and the usual strange Tallahassee government decisions and political situations. All goes well here. What's up?"

"As was predicted, Europa's small mass exerts sufficient gravitational force to slowly pull the Europa Inspector spacecraft into a gradually diminishing orbit around the moon with each flyby. When that happens, at a point, hard decisions have to be made; for once the spacecraft gets to a certain distance from Europa it can't escape the gravitational pull of the moon with its small attitude thruster units and will crash into the moon," transmitted Berks.

"Because of the potential for contamination of the moon's pristine environment with Earth organisms, this is not acceptable. Hera-

Juno, as you know, there may be some sort of life on this moon. We can't take a chance of introducing any of Earth's life forms, giving the illusion of actual Europan life."

Quickly reviewing the data they had sent, Hera-Juno responded, "I'm aware of that and have been monitoring the increasing gravitational pull myself. I knew that this was critical before I got close to the Falcon Heavy rocket at KSC and transported myself into the spacecraft's memory. While the thought of pulling away from Europa toward Jupiter and ending up being a brief puff of dissipating energy absorbed by old Jupiter is spooky, at least I will be able to observe Jupiter from close up. Although its radiation will probably fry Inspector's electronics, with me electronically stored inside before I got there.

"Berks, your concern is appreciated. I'll just hold out here until the last moment. I've made some calculations as to how much longer I have before exiting Europa. Let's see what you have."

"Eddie here. I can't believe Berks called me 'Old Eddie'; this project has turned his hair gray, what there is left on his shiny, old fuzzball.

"According to the data you have been sending to us, that of the gradual increase in gravitational pull and the changes in your orbit, we believe that you have about 3.25 Earth weeks left, perhaps a bit more."

"Agrees closely with my calculations," transmitted Hera-Juno. "Let's get ready for Inspector's eventual ejection from Europa's orbit. However, best we do that by providing me with a software upgrade with plans for my observational activities as I approach Jupiter. I'll modify the hardware's software for that purpose."

"We'll get with the project scientists on that. Part of it has already been done. However, we need to input your projected departure date from Europa," transmitted Berks.

Pausing, "We are both sorry we can't help you."

"No worries, guys. Until then, I'll take a further look at what you sent and provide input as needed. Meanwhile, I'll continue observing Europa."

Well, it was my decision. Life on earth had become so boring. I needed to do something different. And, I needed to get away from DARPA.

Suck it up, old girl. What happens now is out of your control. You got yourself on this spacecraft; live with it. Live? How about dying?

*Europa Clipper is the NASA name for the spacecraft to be launched from KSC in October 2024

In this novella, it is called Europa Inspector.

CHAPTER TWO

Jupiter

Every time Hera-Juno looked at Jupiter, a "chill" ran through Inspector's computer memory bank. The planet was so large, with an enormous red eyeball, the Great Red Spot, staring angrily at her within its horizontal bands of beautiful, visible-light, pastel-colored cloud layers.

If I have to smash into Jupiter, I want to poke right into that mean red eye!

Having finished a planned flyby of Europa, the spacecraft was entering its data-transfer mode to NASA. She had nothing to do at the moment.

She stared:

It was monstrous, with a mass 2.5 times that of all the other planets in the Solar System, combined. Much larger than Earth it, however, is much less dense, being comprised of gas and liquid, rather than solid matter.

Randomly, as the spacecraft went through its elliptical paths preparing for another flyby, she spotted the other large moons, Callisto, Ganymede, and Io. There were 95 official moons (79 less than 10 km in diameter) by 2022, with many thousands of other unnamed objects, perhaps captured asteroids or fragments of such asteroids, orbiting Jupiter. And, although there was a planetary ring system, she could not see it.

It's magnificent, but I hate it.

Hera-Juno knew that she would soon have a close relationship with Jupiter, a very short one, a deadly one.

CHAPTER THREE

A Backward Glance

Mumbling to herself in Europa Inspector's computer memory bank, Hera-Juno reflected on what faced her in a few weeks: *Forever Death.*

Berks and Eddie didn't need to remind her. She was riding a fast-moving arrow of time, with a waiting, voracious Jupiter being the target.

She had had a good life, both in her electronic and her meat-person forms. Living longer would be preferred, but her decision to "jump" to the Europa Inspector spacecraft before launch had been her choice, one she didn't regret.

Yes, *meat-person,* for she had once been a live human being.

She recalled what had happened to bring her to live in the spacecraft.

Close to ten years ago:

Milo Herskovitz sat at the kitchen table in his small lakeside house in Dorado, Florida, listening to Missus Gurley's chatter. He smiled. She so loved to talk.

Speaking from the super-cellphone resting on a shelf above the table, she looked from the screen at Milo.

"Milo, I'm bored to death! Wait, that's funny, at least in a morbid sort of way. I'm already dead, somewhat," laughing.

"Excuse me, Missus Gurley," said Milo, who was pouring and slurping the last of the milk in the uplifted breakfast cereal bowl into his wide-open mouth. "What's so funny about that, being dead?"

"Being bored to death? Well, here I am, living inside a

cellphone. Yes, living, alive! Yet, my body, that of Emily Sue Barker, the real me, is buried under a red granite tombstone in Hills of Heaven Cemetery here in Dorado, Florida, across the street from the Clucking Chicken restaurant, just down the road from your house. I would hate to see what my old meat-person looks like after so many years of decay. I can't believe that they dug me up for DNA testing, and then buried me again."

Missus Gurley had come into Milo's life, in ways both normal and abnormal.

Arriving in Dorado, finally working up the nerve to escape a domineering family and, in particular, an over-bearing, obnoxious maiden aunt in Fort Lauderdale, he had opened a small computer sales and repair store in Thompson, the county-seat of Gulf-coastal Mann County, Florida.

Supplementing that meager income, he helped older, less tech-savvy residents resolve computer and software problems, and taught computer skills at retirement centers.

Missus Gurley, lonely, and seemingly incompetent in the mysterious world of computers, had contacted Milo, refusing to go to such classes, asking for private tutoring. Over many years, she and Milo became very close.

After her unexpected death, she, to Milo's surprise, had willed her lakeside house, a small, red pickup truck, and a great sum of money and mutual funds to him. He and his dog, Chompy, moved in.

Milo often regretted that he had never visited Missus Gurley's grave since the burial. He loved her but had focused so much on running his store and the computer classes, even though he constantly missed her.

One day, impulsively reacting to an impossible story told by Oscar Ramos, the owner of the small, family-owned Mexican restaurant next to his store, he thought he might try to do the same, although he had thought it nonsense.

Over several cold *Tecate* beers and tortilla chips and salsa for dipping, Oscar had recounted how his beloved, elderly mother would often go to the old cemetery next to the church in her small mountain village near Puebla, Mexico, where her husband and others were buried and, placing her forehead on the hard tombstones, listen and speak to the dead.

So, nervously, late in an evening when no one was in Hills of Heaven Cemetery, Milo had crept into it, curious as to whether Missus Gurley could hear him if he were to try the same. Tentatively pressing an ear onto her cold, red-granite tombstone, he heard a low buzzing.

Later, assembling a mix of jury-rigged devices he made from a pile of surplus computers and surplus Radio Shack electronics he had in his shop, and using special audio-editing software, he returned to the gravesite and was able to record and later decipher the rhythmic, yet random, buzzing, hearing Missus Gurley speaking to him.

Although she was dead, some residuum of her life spirit had sensed his presence, responding. He could not answer her but listened to the detailed instructions she gave him.

Recovering a strange-looking cellphone and a notebook from a metal box buried in a corner of a shed at the house she had willed to him, he did what she had written in the notebook.

Missus Gurley turned out not to be the computer-challenged old lady he had thought. She was an artificial-intelligence and robotics expert, a brilliant mind, having designed the special cellphone into which she had, before dying, uploaded herself, hoping for further life.

Charging and turning on the phone, and entering a password he found in the notebook, it accessed a sophisticated program called MIND, which Milo activated. This uploaded Missus Gurley's memories and personality from the previous storage in the cellphone.

She was then ALIVE, living within the cellphone. Stunned, he could see her move on the cellphone screen, and talk to her.

When he first saw her face on the screen, she was as she had been when young, very attractive. As she said to Milo when he first saw her, "Why should I come back as an old woman? Why not the way I looked when much younger? What do you think? Like you young fellows say, hot?"

However, she realized that her youthful appearance was unreasonable, so she reverted to being a seventy-plus-year-old woman on the screen, the one that Milo had known and loved.

Most of the time, Milo carried the modified super-cellphone in his left shirt pocket, the camera lens looking out of a wide hole he had cut in his shirt so that she could see what was going on. He wore an earbud to listen to her, which he was doing now as he put the bowl and coffee cup in the sink for later washing.

"Yes, Emily Sue Barker. I almost forgot your real name. It's hard to comprehend all that we have gone through. To me, you will always be Elizabeth Anne Gurley, Missus Gurley."

"And, you will always be my Milo. I feel like you are the son I never had. Wish I could hug you."

"Me too," said Milo.

Smiling, she responded, "Yes, what changes there have been in my life, our lives. DARPA agents, the US Defense Advanced Research Projects Agency, verified that I was dead. When they barged into the cemetery, flashing badges and papers with official seals, they dug up my coffin and took samples for DNA analysis. They found me, Emily Sue Barker, my decaying body. I'm dead as far as they know. At least that part is past, I hope. One never knows if they will show up again. They can be so tenacious."

Despite the slow-witted, little old lady appearance she had presented to others when was alive as a physical human being, she was a very intelligent person. As a child, she was considered to be a genius; didn't like being called one, and just wanted to be a regular kid, playing with others.

However, people wouldn't let her be one, never had a true childhood, friends, fun, and games. She kept moving forward from grade to grade, skipping some, and went from one level of schooling to another, far faster than her peers. Before she knew it, she had two PhDs, one in applied physics and the other in early computer engineering and programming, along with some experimental robotics, all at age twenty-one.

At that time, despite those feelings about her upbringing, she focused on robots and artificial intelligence (AI). She became quite skilled in those two fields; people noticed. A large household appliance manufacturer, Dream Home (DH), hired her to develop software and robots to work with their products.

One should say semi-robots because that's all they were. Nothing more than household gadgets; blunt, unthinking machines to make life easier for lazy humans with too much money. Such machines simply react to visuals, things they were programmed to detect/see, but just unknowingly follow those programs.

It was the future DH said; can't stop it, and saw it as a way to make money. However, her service-oriented, home robots were much more advanced than the ones DH had been producing before she came; they had a bit of semi-independent intelligence. She was a valued and respected employee.

DARPA, always alert to innovative, perhaps usable technologies, had noted her skills. They "forced" a meeting with her and DH, essentially stealing her away to work on DARPA's projects, wanting to link AI and robotics.

Working for DARPA, it became obvious to her that human-intelligence and machine-intelligence could be blended, and linked together, directly. Yet, what they wanted to do was to implant active working, remotely-situated human brains into war machines. She could not go along with this. She feared for the mental, even physical, loss of the lives of young people they would be using.

She ran away from DARPA, coming to small-town Dorado, located in west-coast peninsular Florida, inland from the Gulf of Mexico. She refused to be part of such horrors. Here, she hid out, changed her name to Elizabeth Anne Gurley, and eventually met Milo. DARPA stopped searching for her when they verified that it was Emily Sue Barker's body, her real name, in the cemetery.

Suddenly, she burst into electronic laughter, thinking about Mann County's sheriff, Ephraim Johnson:

I still feel sorry for the poor guy. Sheriff Johnson was so incompetent in resolving the crimes in his jurisdiction. He was fortunate that I was around to help him. Johnson thought it was Milo meddling in his affairs, when, using the Internet, I broke through his so-called computer firewall to see what he was doing. He had no idea I was inside the cellphone Milo carried with him.

Even before I left, he and Milo would have their Friday morning weekly sausage gravy and biscuits breakfast together at the Clucking Chicken, with me watching them from the cellphone in Milo's shirt pocket.

And, Milo, so timid, was forever frustrated with my nosing into Sheriff Johnson's business. I had to do it, or none of the crimes would have been resolved. It was such fun and challenging being a detective, as well as breaking into the Sheriff's Office computer and providing Johnson with the clues he needed.

My favorite cases were the murdered fisherman on Lake Atcheanahoe near Dorado, Florida, and the four skulls case at the Manatee Center in coastal Clear River. The Mirror Lake Retirement Village murder near Flowertown was a hard one. The Orangeland Paddlewheeler coin theft and murder at Little Big River was a bit messy, with an innocent party almost getting the blame.

And, that last one, where the lonely, homely woman furiously stabbed a man who pretended to be in love with her. Right in the Mann County museum's historical document storage room in Thompson. Blood was everywhere and the woman screaming and screaming, not knowing what she had done, her brain twisted by the hate for his treachery.

I will always be thankful for Milo helping me build a robot to move around in. Well, I wasn't physically inside it ... just had the cellphone, me inside, attached to its neck. However, what freedom!

After that, I realized I needed a new life, so I hopped onto the Europa Inspector spacecraft for a joy ride. No, I knew what I was doing, and, here I am, on my way to dying.

Oh, well. Back to work. Have to get ready for the next flyby. Never know what I might see.

CHAPTER FOUR

Jupiter's Moon Europa

Before hitching a ride on the Europa Inspector spacecraft as it launched from KSC on a Falcon Heavy rocket, Hera-Juno, at that time being old Missus Gurley, spent time on the Internet researching and preparing herself for the one-way trip. She wanted to know what she was in for, and what background she needed.

She prepared herself for the trip as a "stowaway" in the memory storage banks of the Europa Inspector spacecraft by learning as much as she could about the strategy of the project, the power and propulsion of the spacecraft, and the rocket, the launch and trajectory of the spacecraft, and, most important, the scientific package. This latter was most vital, as she thought she was likely to become involved in its operation.

The goals of the Europa Inspector spacecraft are to explore the moon Europa, investigate its potential for or presence of life, and aid in the selection of a landing site for the future *Europa Lander*. This exploration focuses on the three main requirements for life: liquid water, chemistry, and energy. Specifically, the objectives are to study:

Ice shell and ocean: Confirm the existence, and characterize the nature, of water within or beneath the ice, and processes of surface-ice-ocean exchange.

Composition: Distribution and chemistry of key compounds and the links to ocean composition.

Geology: Characteristics and formation of surface features, including sites of recent or current activity.

In summary:

Europa is the smallest of the four Galilean moons, discovered in 1610 by Galileo Galilei, orbiting Jupiter, and the sixth closest moon to Jupiter. Its diameter is 1,900 miles, slightly smaller than Earth's Moon. It orbits Jupiter in just over three-and-a-half Earth days. One hemisphere of the moon always faces the planet, gravitationally locked-in that position by massive Jupiter. However, as it approaches Jupiter, Europa elongates slightly, then relaxes as it moves away, having been "kneaded" by Jupiter.

The Jupiter flybys of Pioneer 10 and 11 in 1973 and 1974, respectively, acquired very low-resolution photos. So, at that point, researchers knew little of Europa. In 1979 the two Voyager spacecraft passed through the Jovian (Jupiter) system, providing the first hints that Europa might contain liquid water or slushy ice. It is thought that Europa has a 10 to 15-mile-thick ice shell floating on an ocean 40 to 100 miles deep. Additionally, Europa is likely to have an iron-nickel core and a rocky silicate mantle overlain by an ocean of salty (chloride) water.

Long linear features, often surface-stained by a reddish-brown material whose composition is not certain, but may contain salts such as magnesium sulfate and reddish sulfur compounds, crisscross Europa's water-ice surface. These fractures are only about a mile or more wide but hundreds of miles long. The fractures have built up into tall ridges. And, some of the fractures have been pulled apart into smaller parallel fractures. Further determination of this surface material's composition may provide more information as to the moon's potential as a life-bearing world. And, that is the main focus for sending an exploratory spacecraft to the moon.

The 1995-2003 NASA Galileo spacecraft also, in flybys, revealed pits and domes that suggested that Europa's ice layer could be slowly churning, convecting, due to an unknown heat source from below. This warmer ice-water would rise like Earth's magma rising through overlying rocks.

A later reanalysis of the data collected by the Galileo spacecraft suggested that small plumes of water may be ejecting up to 160 miles above the icy surface of Europa. This was spectrographically confirmed as water vapor in November 2019 by the Keck Observatory in Hawaii. Otherwise, Europa's atmosphere is thin and tenuous, primarily composed of non-biological oxygen and trace amounts of water vapor, perhaps extending up to 100 miles above the surface.

Because of this, researchers thought that an exploratory spacecraft could pass through one of Europa's water plumes and sample it, thus analyzing the composition of the moon's ocean. The Cassini spacecraft previously did this for Saturn's moon, Enceladus, which also has an ocean spewing water into space.

It is believed that as Jupiter exerts its strong gravitational pull on Europa, the thick ice shell is being subjected to distortion and flexes from these periodic tidal forces, allowing warmer and less-dense ice to rise from depths, and be released as volumes of water, the plumes. Such analyzed water would help to determine whether Europa's ocean might be hospitable for some form of life. Maneuvering a spacecraft through one of these episodic plumes may be difficult.

While the presence of water with the right chemical elements is likely, for life to form, an energy source is needed. What this source on Europa might be is unknown. However, on Earth, life-forms have been thriving near submarine volcanoes and deep-sea geothermal vents. These life-forms are called *extremophiles* for the extreme environment they live in. Similar life-forms may live near such energy sources on Europa. The flexing of Europa's seafloor by Jupiter's gravitational pull may result in such possible hydrothermal activity. In addition, there is the possibility of *endoliths,* life-forms living within the rocky mantle materials above the iron-nickel core, as they do on Earth. Another possibility is that they live on the underside of Europa's ice layer, like algae and bacteria in Earth's Polar Regions.

CHAPTER FIVE

Hera-Juno's Past

Hera-Juno attentively watched the cracked and rumpled, whitish and, sometimes, bluish and brownish surface of Europa passing beneath her with feed from the E-THEMIS, MISE, EIS, EUROPA-UVS (appendix), and other observational and data-collection systems as Inspector made another of the four years of planned forty-five close flybys.

Nothing new, except that last flyby when the SUDA caught some particles in the atmosphere of Europa. NASA was quite excited to receive that data.

No new fractures or additional water plumes. Geologic events are far apart. Yet, that she was here in the spacecraft seeing all of this was still overwhelming.

Then, as she looked at the data coming in, from her memory, up popped the loving faces of Milo and Rosalie, and even that silly dog, Chompy. What secrets Milo had kept from Rosalie! Yet, she had had to know about me and my past.

With an electronic twitch, she recalled the events of more than six years ago leading to her being on Europa Inspector.

***

"Milo, it's time to let Rosalie know what's going on. She needs to know about me," said Missus Gurley, known to Rosalie only as Liz. She thought that Liz on the cellphone was a friend of Milo's, not a person living in the device.

Rosalie McGrath, the Goth girl he met in Clear River, had recently moved in with Milo. She had been a docent at the Manatee Center.

"Why? All of a sudden. I don't understand," said Milo, relaxing on the couch.

"I can't hang around here any longer. DARPA is getting too close, ready to spring a trap. You will be in it, along with me. I can't let this happen.

"Rosalie might also get hurt. I'm not talking about physically but from their national security approach. To keep things like me secret, they can ruin reputations."

"What's going on that this has to be done now?" said Milo, laying down a well-read copy of *PC Magazine*.

Waving her arms about on the cellphone, "I'm going to leave the cellphone I live in and go on a rocket to Europa."

Laughing, "Leave the cellphone? A rocket? To Europe? Which country?"

"No, no. I'm serious. Europa is one of the moons of Jupiter. That's why I was so happy to go on our recent trip with you and Rosalie to see the Space Center and the launch areas. Such a fun trip, with me attached to the neck of the robot, talking to the kids.

"It helped me to see the situation there. I have a plan for transferring myself to the computer memory bank of the Europa Inspector spacecraft. When it takes off, I'll be gone. Then, DARPA can't reach me or have a reason to get to you two."

"Is this another one of your crazy ideas? Are you serious? You are always up to something, with me getting in trouble."

"Milo, very much so. I'm committed to leaving Earth. I must. They are so close. You know that they have been snooping around. You've seen them, and I've pointed them out. It could happen any day."

Sitting up, "Leaving? I wasn't expecting something like this. However, you have my support. And, yes, we'll need to tell Rosalie."

"I need both you and Rosalie to help me. There is not much time before the launch. I want to be ready before then. I can't do what has to be done by myself. However, I can tell you what to do."

"So, soon?"

"Yesterday if possible. I can't wait."

"OK, I'll tell her, with your help."

***

"I don't believe it. You and Liz are having fun with me, aren't you, Milo?" her face screwed up, incredulous.

Not smiling. Standing in front of her, Milo reached out, holding onto Rosalie's shoulders, and looking into her eyes.

"This is not a fun thing. She needs our help."

Turning the cellphone on its stand toward Rosalie, he said, "Liz, you asked me to do this. However, I think it would be best that you tell Rosalie what this is all about."

Looking intently from the cellphone screen, "Rosalie, I know that what Milo briefly told you seems impossible. However, it is one hundred percent true. I am Milo's friend you know as Liz. My name is, as Milo calls me, Missus Gurley, Elizabeth Anne Gurley.

"I am dead, except that I live inside the memory components of this special cellphone I designed. My human body is in the cemetery across from the Clucking Chicken restaurant. The granite tombstone says Elizabeth Anne Gurley. My real name is Emily Sue Barker. You can still call me Liz if you want to.

Now, let me tell you about myself and my relationship with Milo."

Rosalie shook her head back and forth, scowling at Milo for pulling such a trick.

What is this nonsense?

Slowly, Missus Gurley told her story. However, watching for her reaction, she sensed that Rosalie didn't believe her, that she and Milo were pulling an elaborate stunt.

She was about to give up, as, seemingly, there was no easy way for Rosalie to believe her and Milo.

Then it came to her what to do.

"Milo, clip the cellphone on top of the robot."

He removed it from the stand, walked over to the chair where the robot sat, and snapped it in place, making the necessary connections.

Looking out from the cellphone screen, "Rosalie, does Milo have the robot controller in his hands?

'No? Where is it?"

"It's on that bookcase shelf."

"Is it turned on?"

"I don't know."

"Pick it up. Take the batteries out."

Walking over, "OK, they are out."

"Does Milo have a second controller? Does he have one in his hands?"

"No."

"Now, if the robot were to be controlled by Milo, what would he need to do to make it walk about?"

"He'd have the controller in his hand and push the command buttons like he always does."

"And, if the robot would now walk across the room to hug you, what would you do?"

Putting her hands on her cheeks, mouth open, "Probably scream. It's impossible."

"Lay the inactive controller on the floor. Yes, like that.

"I have always wanted to give you a big hug. You and Milo are my best friends. I will never forget you guys. However, there is something I must do. I have already spoken to Milo about it. He will explain it to you, as I will also. Your help is needed for it to be successful."

The robot got up from the chair where it had been resting; arms outstretched, and walked to a gawking Rosalie, who had backed away, having dropped her arms slack to her sides, stumbling.

It embraced Rosalie fondly, with the hum of servos.

At first, Rosalie was frozen in the metal arms. Then, looking into the cellphone screen, seeing Missus Gurley's face she started to cry. She struggled with the metal arms and hugged the robot.

"I can't believe what's happening," said Rosalie. "It must be real. There is no way that a robot could run itself, and hug me with such a feeling unless someone was inside it. Are you real?" staring at the screen.

"As real as you and Milo, except that I'm only a collection of my life's memories in this cellphone, not a physical person. I am a dead person. I build on those memories, just as you do. I have feelings, emotions, and many human needs, except for physical things like food and a good glass of wine to go with it. Sadly, I cannot feel your hug.

"At the same time, there is a chance that I will never die. I am the first of my kind. However, there may be others like me in the future."

Turning to look at him, "Milo, we have to move much faster. You messed up at the Kennedy Space Center complex when you took me to see all of the rockets and exhibits," said Missus Gurley.

"What? How?"

"A couple of times you were not pushing the cellphone buttons ... yet the robot moved on its own. DARPA saw this."

"They were there? Who?"

"A skinny, red-haired man surreptitiously watching people at the turnstiles. Not sure why he was there. Probably someone tailing you for DARPA. Here's a picture of him, looking at me. He also watched you."

"What can we do?"

"I'm developing plans and schematics for what I need. You will need to get the materials to make the equipment."

"And, Rosalie?"

"She can help you put it together."

***

Milo and Rosalie sat together on the living room couch. Missus Gurley in the cellphone, propped up on the coffee table in front of them, quietly waited for responses to her needs.

"Liz, what is this NASA Europa Inspector spacecraft that you want to go on, and why do you want to go?" said Rosalie.

"Sure, I can explain why I want to go on the Europa Inspector, and what it is.

"The main reason for getting on it is that I have to get out of Dodge".

"Excuse me," said Rosalie. "What's dodge? Are you dodging someone?"

Laughing, "Actually, yes. It comes from an old TV show, *Gunsmoke*. It was said by Marshall Matt Dillon to the bad guys. "Get the hell out of Dodge", meaning get out of Dodge City, Kansas or you'll pay a price.

"For me, it means leaving Earth, getting away from the bad guys that want me, for my knowledge of artificial intelligence, DARPA.

"Now, as Milo may have told you, many questions arose about Europa, one of Jupiter's moons, after the Galileo spacecraft's long orbiting of Jupiter. The spacecraft I will be on if I can get into it, will be going into a series of elliptical orbits around Jupiter and making forty-five close flybys of the moon, observing and collecting data.

"The scientific payload of the spacecraft will have nine instrumented components. I won't go into detail of what they will do, but here they are:

- Thermal emissions imaging system
- Mapping imaging spectrometer
- Europa imaging system
- Europa ultraviolet Spectrograph
- Radar Europa assessment and sounding: ocean to near-surface
- Europa magnetometer
- Plasma instrument for magnetic sounding
- Mass spectrometer for planetary exploration
- Surface dust analyzer

"Rosalie and Milo, these scientific modules will be active or used during different flybys. For detailed discussions of each one, check NASA on the Internet. They are too complicated to explain.

"Flybys, using gravity assists from Europa, Ganymede, and Callisto are employed to reduce the exposure of the spacecraft and its instrumentation to the intense radiation from Jupiter's magnetosphere, swinging way out beyond Jupiter, and then coming in close for a quick flyby of the moon."

"What will you do on the spacecraft?" said Milo.

"I'm not sure. I'll work on that later. My main goal is to get off Earth so that DARPA can't get me or bother the two of you. Beyond that, I'll be checking out the spacecraft and its scientific packages.

"Maybe I can be helpful to the NASA team of researchers. Distant spacecraft often have problems. You can't bring them back to the repair shop for adjustments. So, engineers on Earth have to communicate long-distance with them to make changes or corrections to the software. Being on-site, I might be able to detect problems and even make the necessary changes, faster. My skills with computers, software, and robotics might be useful. It's super exciting to think about!"

"What about the radiation from Jupiter? I've read about that. Aren't you concerned?"

"Of course I am. However, I'll have several years before the 100-meter-wide solar panels providing energy are damaged by ionizing radiation. It's better than staying here with the DARPA vultures. I'll figure out a way to overcome that situation. Not to worry.

"As far as radiation harming me, a thick wall of a titanium-aluminum alloy will surround me in a vault, and I'll be deep in the spacecraft's interior, hopefully protected. My mind will be in the Europa Inspector's electronics, something quite sensitive to Jupiter's radiation. Its magnetosphere is fourteen times stronger than Earth's and generates radiation equivalent to 100 million X-rays. Do you see my concern?"

"So, you might be able to operate the spacecraft? Wow!" said Milo.

Laughing, Missus Gurley said, "Maybe, maybe not. I won't know what I can do until I'm on board. If I make it, I'll take a look at NASA's spacecraft programs before launch. Then, being, essentially, software myself, I'll become part of their programs. That's if I can blend into it, and be compatible. I have been doing a lot of research on the Internet, much of it related to the operation of the on-board equipment.

"In a sense, I'll be in the *driver's seat*. Yes, Milo, I'll be the Captain of the spacecraft.

"Internet research indicates that the spacecraft will not be going directly to Jupiter, but after launch will use gravitational assists from Mars and Earth to achieve the velocity needed to get there, rather than depending completely upon its propulsion. However, the spacecraft has 24 rocket engines to initially propel it on its trajectory, once it leaves Earth's atmosphere.

"Maybe that's NASA's plan, to eventually use these engines to avoid contamination of Europa's water with Earth organisms. That's what they did with Galileo in 2003.

"However, I've been looking into options, such as using the small iodine-ion thrusters that the spacecraft has for slight changes in attitude and altitude when it arrives at Europa and for the flybys."

***

"Milo, I'm considering a variety of transfer devices for me to access the memory components of the Europa Inspector payload. I know only a little about the nature of the materials comprising the nose cone/cargo bay of the rocket. Therefore, I don't have an idea as to what wavelengths I might need to penetrate that material. If I can get through the nose cone with a certain wavelength, I should be able to get inside the spacecraft's computer.

"However, the nose cone/fairings are likely to be metals or with too much metal in them. If that's the case, I can't get through.

"My efforts will eat up a lot of the money that I gave you. Is that OK? We have no choice, short of electronic suicide on my part."

"Missus Gurley, the money means nothing to us," said Milo. "I have my store, and Rosalie and her mother are opening a coffee shop/bookstore and vinyl collectors shop in Thompson. It's your money, not mine."

"Good. There should be quite a bit left. What I gave you is, in large part, invested in stable mutual funds.

"DARPA is too close. I have to get into that spacecraft. I have to leave Earth.

"When they use the crawler to roll the rocket out of the Assembly Complex to the launchpad, I'll be able to test the devices we will be building. If one of the radio wavelengths works, I'll take a "walk" inside its computer memory and storage components, trying to understand its makeup.

"If it looks like I can get in and determine that I can manipulate the spacecraft once it is in the Europa flyby stages, then I'll make the transfer. My success won't be known until six years later, sometime in 2030. I will attempt to communicate with you and the world when I get there. I dare not make contact at any time before that."

"Here's a list of what I'm going to need."

"Won't DARPA be watching me buy this stuff?" said Milo.

"Certainly, they will. However, what I want to do makes no sense to them in terms of the robot and AI. They will be confused. They will have meetings. Such bumblers."

"I hope so," Said Milo.

"We must be quick about this. There is so little time before they show up for the robot and me."

***

"So, what is this that Rosalie and I have built?" said Milo, bent over a metal box with gauges and a long probe on one end.

"The only wavelengths I can use safely and economically are those in the radio range, from short to long wavelengths. I was concerned about focusing the radio waves into a tight beam until I found on the Internet that someone had fabricated a three-dimensional, lightweight metamaterial 'lens' that focuses radio waves with extreme precision. The concave lens they came up with exhibits a property called negative refraction, bending electromagnetic waves, in this case, radio waves, in exactly the opposite sense from which a normal concave lens would work. That's one thing you have made, improved upon the original.

"The researchers found that radio waves converged in front of the lens at a very specific point, creating a tight, focused beam. Ours will use a series of lenses to keep the beam even tighter, over a longer distance than they have tested. This device will focus radio waves into a single, needle-like beam, one that I can use to probe the rocket and the Europa Inspector spacecraft.

"How I'm going to get in is still a big question. I'll know when I try.

"The transfer device you built will move me from the cellphone and place me in the computer memory of the Europa Inspector spacecraft. Once in, I'll explore. I can't reverse the transport to return once I'm in all the way.

"There is danger. I could disappear within an instant if the transfer fails or if I have made the wrong assumptions in the design of the device, or the memory components of the spacecraft. In addition, there will be no way for me to tell you that all went well. I can't communicate until much later, for fear that NASA will notice.

"If my efforts fail, I want another try to do something. Milo, make a backup of this cellphone, just in case."

"I will. Where should I keep it?"

"Not at the house, in case DARPA has a raid, which I expect. Keep it and any others in our secret place, under the pile of old computers and electronics in your store. Also, if they come for the robot, you may have to build another one."

"Got it."

* * *

"Milo, there is one complicating factor concerning my being inside the Europa Inspector spacecraft. I sort of hinted at it earlier. I need to tell you both about it. Would you have Rosalie come inside?"

Chompy, his dog, and Rosalie were madly racing around in the yard, chasing each other. When Milo called her, she came in.

"What's up?"

Milo had a bewildered look on his face, "Missus Gurley wants to tell us something. I don't like the way that she asked me to have both of us present. Must be something serious."

"Yes, it is a, possibly, serious matter. Please sit down. I won't know until much later when I'm in the spacecraft," said Missus Gurley.

"Let me explain to you what NASA's schedule is. It will take close to six years to get from launch into orbit around Jupiter, setting up for the flybys. The flybys will then take place over about four years. All of that is part of a well-designed program. The serious part is what happens to the spacecraft when the scientific work is complete. I sort of mentioned it earlier."

"And, that is what?" said Milo.

"I'm not sure of the estimated time for it to happen. However, to avoid contamination of the ice-waters of Europa with possible organisms from Earth, the plan is to dispose of the spacecraft by allowing it to impact Jupiter, rather than let the gravity of Europa pull it down. If that happens, that is the end for me."

"Oh, no!" said Rosalie, hands to her mouth.

"It looks like a complicated and even horrendous problem. However, I believe I can get around it. If I can, maybe I can avoid being roasted and toasted by a final dive into Jupiter.

"However, to do any of this, I must get into the spacecraft first. Then, I will figure out something. I will find some way to keep going. Nevertheless, rather than the two of you hearing about the intended disposal of the spacecraft in the news, I thought it best to forewarn you and to give you hope that nothing will happen to me."

"How will you do this, survive?" said Milo.

"Milo and Rosalie, it's like watching corny television shows in the 1950s and 1960s.

In a deep voice, *How will our hero overcome the threat from the bad guys? Tune in next week, same time and same channel.*

"So, not to panic. Not to worry."

Milo and Rosalie, shocked, stared into the cellphone, "We hope so."

"Get that look off your faces. Trust me. I always figure things out, or maybe things figure me out, Ha!"

***

It was mid-week, with a bright sun and few clouds. There were only a few people on Titusville Beach to the south of the Kennedy Space Center, mainly joggers and older people. The beach was close to the launchpads for the public to set up chairs to watch.

Wandering retirees, heads down, looking for shells, moved along the shore like sanderlings feeding on sand crabs, amphipods, isopods, insects, marine worms, and small mollusks, avoiding bumping into each other as they scurried back-and-forth with the surge of the waves crashing in and dissipating. Likewise, the older folk with their grabber-tongs picked up their shell treasures, moving about.

"Milo, I'm going to try to access the Europa Inspector spacecraft's computer memory. I'm not sure which method will allow me to get in, so I'll try a range of focused radio wavelengths. That might work. I'll have to penetrate the nose cone where the spacecraft is housed. So, be ready," said Missus Gurley.

"Ready for what?"

"If I get in, and find out what I need to know, I'm staying in. I'll be gone. This device we made will not permit a return."

To avoid any suspicion from others in the area, Milo had parked his old computer shop van at the far north end of the beach parking lot and backed it up toward Launch Complex 39A. The transmission probe that he and Rosalie had built for Missus Gurley extended upward, slightly out of the open back doors. From there, it was a clear but distant view of where the enormous crawler had moved the Falcon Heavy with the Europa Inspector from the assembly building, readying it for launch.

Milo had put a beach chair on top of the van, boosting Rosalie on top.

"Rosalie, I know that this may seem ridiculous, but you have to stay on top of the van, sunning yourself. We have to look innocent."

Looking down, "Me, a Goth girl, in a bright red bikini. So weird! I'll get burned."

"You look hot, sexy. Just lather up with sunscreen."

"Milo, you want a good slapping about?"

"Just doing what has to be done."

Missus Gurley, inside the van, cellphone on top of the robot, was busy. She seemed frustrated.

"This damned USB cable has to connect the cellphone to the transmission probe equipment, Milo. I'll need it to transmit myself to the focusing-processing device and into the spacecraft if the probing works.

"So, connect it for me. I can't get it into the slot."

"OK. It's snapped in place."

Milo, "The probe is not quite centered on the cargo cone. See what you can do. I have been trying to do it with the robot, but its hand sensors can't do the fine work needed."

Milo made a series of small adjustments, "Sure. How about now?"

"Yes, hopefully. Won't know until I try. No idea where in the damned cone the spacecraft is positioned. I'll have to use a wide scan of exploratory transmissions over its surface until I get a response. I may not get anything, but I must try. I'll need your help with this. And, tell Rosalie to not move about. The van can't be rocked."

After about fifteen minutes.

"I can't get into the nose cone. Too much metal. As I expected, the radio waves, even tightly focused, won't penetrate. The wavelengths are just not effective."

"What now?"

"I think there is another way in. Standard cable setups for this type of rocket show that there are at least three cables, probably shielded, carrying an electric current into various parts of the rocket, and maybe to the nose cone.

"I'm running a scan of those cables, moving up and down, looking for some sort of access, maybe a structural weakness. One of them must lead to the spacecraft section, probably the uppermost one. If so, it may have a direct connection to it. I would assume that as the spacecraft is the purpose of the launch, they would be monitoring its health. They would not be using wireless; it has to be through the cables.

"Wait. Hold on. Maybe.

"Yes, Jackpot!

"There it is. I can see it!"

"See it? What?" said Milo.

"Made contact. I got through a small cable-sheathing rupture. The cable was kinked. It's going to be easy. Just like hacking into Sheriff Johnson's computer system. Not as easy, but it seems to be responding to my feelers."

"Feelers?"

"Yes. I'm sort of touching it. Learning how it is accessed by NASA. I'm moving around, seeing what's there. I have to find a place to hide, some memory chip with extra storage, or some other data storage area."

A minute later, "Any luck?"

"Yes, get Rosalie down here."

"Why?"

"I'm leaving. It's time to say goodbye.

"Milo, I don't like this, but I have to do it. I've found my new home. I'll soon break the link to the cellphone.

"NASA may detect my intrusion into their system at any moment. They might block me, or stop the launch. It is now or never.

"Hurry!"

Milo stuck his head over the van's back-door roof, "Rosalie, come down, fast!"

Rosalie came into the van. She saw Missus Gurley and Milo looking at her.

"What's up? Why are you two looking at me?"

Voice choking, "Missus Gurley wants to say goodbye. She's made contact with the spacecraft. She's ready to stay in," said Milo.

"Oh, no. I knew that she had to leave, but ..."

"I'm sorry, Rosalie. I have to do it. Hug me. Even through all of these pieces of metal, I can feel it, I'm sure."

Looking at Missus Gurley, whose cellphone face was covered with tears, she hugged the robot.

Sobbing, "Goodbye, I hope you can find some way to keep in touch."

"I will. I'll find a way. I may have already. Don't worry."

Milo approached the robot.

"It's been a long time, Missus Gurley. We have had a lot of fun, haven't we? I'll miss you so much."

"And I will miss you too, Milo, my boy ... my son. Yes, my son."

Milo, crying, hugged her. The robot hugged back, holding on to him for a long time.

"I love you both. And I'm so glad you found each other. Give Chompy a good scratching for me. I will miss racing about in the robot with him.

"Now, be very still. I'm going to do it."

Milo and Rosalie turned to look at the nose cone of the spacecraft.

Then, they heard the words,

"I'm Out'a Here."

With a crash, the robot collapsed to the floor of Milo's van, cellphone and connections flying against the wall with a clatter.

A wide-eyed Rosalie picked up the cellphone and gave it to Milo. Both looked at it, stunned.

"Milo, she's gone!"

Sadly, looking at it, he turned it off, sniffling.

"Yes. I can't believe it. She's gone, forever."

CHAPTER SIX

Pre-Launch Checks

"We may have a problem with Europa Inspector, Sir," said Berks.

"Damn! How's that?"

"About an hour ago we were checking the spacecraft's software programs, the last check before we proceed with the scheduled launch sequence."

"And?"

"One or two of the operational programs and the data storage seem to be larger than they were when we installed them."

"Is that possible?"

"Don't think so. Checked with personnel having access to the spacecraft's programming; no changes or upgrades made since the spacecraft arrived here at KSC."

"Do you see anything critical?"

"No. Just a mismatch in the memory and storage used by the programs."

"Have you tried to reinstall?"

"We have. Nothing happens. No error or warning message, just this:

ALL OPERATIONS STABLE."

"If that's the case, ignore it if all programs function as designed."

"They do. It's just that slight difference in program data and storage quantity."

"Could the spacecraft have made changes on its own?"

"It may be the result of a SELF CHECK, storing the results for reference."

"That's it then. Proceed with the launch schedule."

"Yes, Sir."

CHAPTER SEVEN

Launch

October 2024

Milo, I know it's a long drive back to the Kennedy Space Center, but I would like to see the launch of the Europa Inspector spacecraft with me in it. It's coming up shortly. Could you come to the storage place to pick me up and take me there?" said the backup Missus Gurley, calling.

"Rosalie and I would like to see it also. Sure. Let's do it."

***

"I'm so jealous of me in the Europa Inspector. Just imagine what it would be like. She's a crazy one doing this."

"Missus Gurley, I can't get used to having multiples of you, and making fun of yourself."

"I could have, somehow, had ongoing communication with her, but we might have been detected by NASA. So, I decided against that because of DARPA."

"Milo, should we go back to Titusville Beach to watch?" said Rosalie.

Running his hands through his big poofy mass of black hair, "No, this launch is a super-hot item for big-time launch watchers. It's likely to be jammed there, being so small, and with so little parking.

"Also, and I'm beginning to think like Missus Gurley, it's best we do not go to where we have been before. DARPA knows we were there, I'm sure.

"We could go to Playalinda Beach, north of the launch area.

However, that's about four miles up from Launch Complex 39A. It would be nice to get closer."

"Let's go over the day before or so, and get a motel room. We have time. Then on launch day, go out to the LC-39 Observation Gantry viewing area at the Space Center. I checked online; you need to get tickets. We need to act quickly," said Rosalie. "That way we would be very close to the launch."

"That's what we'll do," said Milo.

"Milo, before we go, I need to show you how to build a simple, working controller for the robot. You will need it for the showdown with DARPA. They are going to try to get the robot soon. Also, get a regular cell phone to put on the robot, I'll show you how to load the control-mechanism software in it. We need to let them capture it and find out that it is not run by AI, and that a controller is needed," said Missus Gurley.

Looking at the cellphone screen, "So, the robot is going with us to watch the launch?"

"No, we'll leave it at the house, along with the controller. I don't want to attract a crowd at the LC-39 Observation area."

"What will DARPA do then?" said Rosalie.

Smiling from the screen, Missus Gurley laughed, "I suspect they will soon come to your house with a search warrant. Then, they will take the useless robot to their headquarters in Virginia for inspection and testing. Of course, it won't work, except with the controller that they also took."

***

Rosalie got the needed motel reservations, as well as tickets for the LC-39 Observation Gantry viewing area.

They settled in on beach chairs, passing binoculars back and forth, trying to see what was going on at the launchpad where the Falcon Heavy stood in its cradle.

Milo mounted the cellphone holding the backup Missus Gurley on a tripod next to them, as if for taking pictures and videos. She kept up a continuously excited chattering in Milo's earbud.

"Oh, I wish I could talk to me, to wish me good luck."

"Looks like the rocket is close to being launched. That last hold was short," said Milo.

Excited, Missus Gurley said, "Yes, it looks like it's going to be a GO. Listen to what they are saying over the loudspeaker:"

***

T-0:07:30
Go/No Go for
Launch
We have Go
T-0:07:00
Spacecraft on
Internal Power
T-0:07:00
First Stage Heater
Shutdown
T-0:07:00
First Stage ACS
Close-Out
T-0:06:35
Second Stage
Heater Shutdown
T-0:06:25
Falcon to Internal
Power
T-0:06:00
Transfer to
Internal complete
T-0:05:55
Pressurization for
Strongback
Retract
T-0:05:30

Strongback
Cradles Opening
T-0:05:00
Second Stage
Nitrogen Loading
Termination
T-0:04:46
Stage 1 & Stage 2
Auto Sequence
starts
T-0:04:30
Stage 2 Thrust
Vector Control
Test
T-0:04:25
Strongback
Retraction
T-0:04:10
Vehicle Release
Auto Sequence
T-0:03:45
Verify Good Mvac
TVC
T-0:03:40
TEA-TEB Ignition
System Activation
T-0:03:30

Strongback
Retraction
complete
T-0:03:25
Flight Termination
System to Internal
Power
T-0:03:05
Flight Termination
System Armed
T-0:03:00
LOX Topping
Termination
T-0:03:00
Strongback
Securing complete
T-0:02:45
Fuel Trim Valve to
Flight Position
T-0:02:40
FTS Countdown
Sequence
T-0:02:30
Go for Launch
T-0:02:20
Propellant Tank
Pre-Press

T-0:02:00
Range Verification
T-0:02:00
Flight Control to
Self-Alignment
T-0:01:35
Helium Loading
Termination
T-0:01:30
Final Engine
Chilldown, Pre-
Valves/Bleeders
Open
T-0:01:20
Engine Purge

T-0:01:00
Flight Computer to
start-up
T-0:01:00
Pad Deck Water
Deluge System
Activation
T-0:00:55
Second Stage to
Flight Pressure
T-0:00:50
First Stage Thrust
Vector Actuator
Test
T-0:00:40

First Stage to
Flight Pressure
T-0:00:20
All Tanks at Flight
Pressure
T-0:00:15
Arm Pyrotechnics
T-0:00:10
Latest VC Abort
T-0:00:03
Merlin Engine
Ignition
T-0:00:00

Then, loudly, over the observation area speakers came:

WE HAVE LIFTOFF!

The distant roar of the Falcon Heavy taking off rolled over them with a deep bone-shaking rumble.

Out of the white cloud of burnt propellant rose a tall silver object on a tower of blinding white flame, the rocket, with the Europa Inspector in its nose cone.

"Damn, look at it go. Have fun other me. Let us know how it went," yelled Missus Gurley.

"Jeez, that hurt," Milo yanked the earbud out.

Angling the cellphone upward as the rocket went, Milo and Rosalie, heads tilted back, gawked at the phenomenal display of power.

The rocket continued to rise, slowly arcing eastward, starting to disappear in a wispy cloud over the Atlantic Ocean.

They watched until the rocket could no longer be seen.

Trying not to cry, Milo looked at Rosalie, "She's gone. Missus

Gurley is going to Europa."

Reaching out to hold his hand, "Yes, she is. I can't believe it. It's unimaginable that this is happening, even though we can no longer see the rocket."

Missus Gurley piped up from the cell phone, "Hey, I'm here. Still alive. Stop bawling!"

That helped a bit, but Milo is still worried. Did she survive? He and Rosalie wait. At what point will someone say all is OK?

"Missus Gurley, do you know when the nose cone/fairings will come off?" said Milo.

"I don't know. That's in their sequences. It will probably be soon. It's something I don't have access to. We'll just have to wait for the announcement.

Continuing to listen to the NASA loudspeaker they heard that the separations were successful and that the nose cone with the Europa Inspector had separated and was moving independently under its power.

"Let's get back to Dorado. We can wait there for further news. I'm sure that all went well, that she will make contact with us, somehow."

CHAPTER EIGHT

After the Launch

Unknown to Hera-Juno on the Europa Inspector, back on Earth:

Driving back to the town of Dorado, not talking, Milo suddenly remembered.

"Rosalie, get Missus Gurley's backup phone out of my camera bag. She wanted to know if it was a success."

Turning it on, they saw her.

"Hello, Milo and Rosalie. How did it go?"

Rosalie responded, as Milo was driving, "We don't know yet. Just what you saw at the launch. We won't know anything until you in the spacecraft contact us. So, I guess we have to wait. She said that it would be later during the flybys of Europa, in 2030, six years from now. Such a long time to wait."

"Even for me, this is strange. It's all about me doing things that I don't know I'm doing because I'm in two places at the same time. I'm so envious of her. She gets to go on a big ride into space", said Missus Gurley, laughing.

"So, what now?" said Rosalie.

"Like I told you," said Missus Gurley. "Once it is confirmed that I'm alive and well in the spacecraft, you will have to turn off all backup phones. Then, smash them with a hammer, get in your kayaks, and paddle out into the lake where one of the flooded sinkholes is located. You know which one I'm talking about, the 50-foot-deep one. At the far end of the lake.

"Casually drop everything into the water. DARPA is not likely to be watching. If they are, that won't matter; it will settle into the corrosive, organic dark muck at the bottom."

"It's still like killing you," said Rosalie.

"Nonsense! Which cellphone has the real me in it? Smashed, none. The only one that counts is me in the Europa Inspector spacecraft."

"We'll do it, but it won't be fun," said Milo.

"I have an option. Once I know that all is well and that I'm OK in the Europa Inspector, I'll access and run a DELETE program on all the phones in storage. That will eliminate any trace of me, including the one I run the delete program from. That way, if you turn on a phone, I will no longer be there.

"Hello, Hello? Nobody Home.

"Then, you can destroy the phones without thinking you are killing me. How does that sound?"

Milo, with a gloomy look on his face, responded, "Much better, except that you will still be gone."

"No, I'll just be way out there near Jupiter, doing flybys of Europa."

"Stop being so miserable, Milo," said Rosalie, "Let's have fun with Missus Gurley while she is still with us. Anything else, Liz?"

"Yes, there is. When you dump the cellphones, take the transmission device and any leftover parts we used for the insertion. Disassemble it. Smash everything.

"Dump them into the underwater sinkhole as well. Burn all the plans and schematics. Delete all emails and parts order information from your computer. Can't delete credit card info or records at the places where orders were made, but that may be enough. Some of this they may be able to recover. If anyone comes, asking, play dumb, both of you.

"Milo, when we get back to Dorado, get a small self-storage rental, out of town. One with a power outlet where you can keep me charged and which has office Wi-Fi which I can access. Take all of the cellphones, including this one, along with all of the probing equipment, and store them there. Don't come to see me. Can't take the risk of you being followed.

"The storage is in case I need to try again. You can keep in touch with me on your phone. I can keep busy poking around on the Internet.

"When we hear from me in Europa, start the disposal process. OK?"

"Sure. Still sounds horrible to us," said Rosalie.

"The cellphone I'm in will be a dead one. I'll be gone."

"Love you, Missus Gurley," said Milo.

"Both of you, too. Say hello, now and then."

CHAPTER NINE

On My Way

Missus Gurley, "strapped in", in the nose cone on top of the Falcon Heavy rocket, waits for the launch of the Europa Inspector spacecraft. She mentally follows what she thinks to be the pre-flight check made by NASA, although she has no access to their computer-controlled launch, can't hear anything, and can't see anything outside of the triangular-shaped fairings of the silver nose cone with its NASA logo.

Nothing happening, yet. According to my calculations, today should be the day. Hoping no holds, so far. If so, that would mean the weather is good. If so, the launch will go as planned.

Calm down. All you can do it wait.

I guess Milo and Rosalie will be watching. Wow, crazy to think about it; I will also be there with them, watching.

Laughing, *What a life and after-life I have had. If this was in a science-fiction book, it would be a big seller. Too bad I can't share this experience with Milo; he would love it.*

She felt a slight buzzing in the electronics. Feedback to the computer where she was stored?

Yes, this is it. They should be counting down.

The countdown must have ended. The Falcon Heavy seemingly launched. She felt a slight static run through the computer's memory bank, but no G-force. No way that a bunch of computer chips could feel that.

Perhaps more feedback from the electronics? This has to be it. I'm on my way to Europa.

Somewhere, down there, Milo and Rosalie are watching. Along with my other me. Hope they enjoy seeing the ride I'm getting. I certainly am, but quite sad as well. Forever gone is a long time.

Ok, the Roll & Pitch Maneuver should be occurring now, according to the planned routines that I found on the Internet. The roll maneuver allows the rocket to align itself to its launch azimuth while the rocket pitches over to perform a gravity turn which allows the rocket to set it on its intended trajectory and assist it in accelerating to orbital speed.

Damn, I'm on my way for sure. Wish I could see what's going on. I don't have access to the cameras that are small bumps on the interstage and the second stage of the rocket.

Anyway, at approximately T+80 seconds (1 minute and 20 seconds after launch), the rocket will go supersonic, meaning it is traveling faster than the speed of sound or has surpassed Mach 1.

Cool! No problems yet, or I would know it. Or, maybe not if the rocket blew. Stop thinking like that!

I'm now at T+90 seconds, MaxQ, with the vehicle passing through the area of maximum dynamic pressure. During this period, the rocket experiences the biggest gravitational pull & most drag while achieving maximum thrust, which puts an incredible amount of stress on the vehicle's structure. Hope it holds together!

Not sure, but it seems that the launch vehicle is powering its thrusters slightly down during this period to reduce the stress on the vehicle. I feel some sort of change in the feedback.

Now we are shortly after MaxQ, at approximately T+3 minutes, the propellants of the first stage are depleted, and the vehicle is powering down its first-stage boosters in preparation for First Stage Separation. That's MECO (Main Engine Cut Off).

Here it comes, if my timing is correct. The First Stage section of the rocket is separating from the rest of the vehicle at T+3 minutes and 30 seconds by detonating explosive bolts or pneumatic systems on the vehicle's interstage. The rocket's interstage connects the different stages of the rocket.

There it goes, jettisoned. Now the rocket's second stage is igniting its engine to carry its payload to the next position at T+4 minutes. Again the electronic vibration, feedback.

After performing a burn for a predetermined period, the second stage engine is shutting down, SECO (Second Engine Cut Off).

The rocket is delivering its payload, the Europa Inspector with me in it, to its predetermined trajectory, first heading toward Mars.

Finally, I might get to see something. However, before an orbital rocket can release or deploy its cargo, it needs to jettison its payload fairing away. The payload fairing is the outer covering or shell of the cargo bay and often also forms the nose cone of a rocket. I'm in the spacecraft behind the fairing.

Here we go. The two halves of the fairing are separating horizontally away from the rocket. There they go. And, there's the release of the second stage. I'm on my way to Europa, after a few side trips, as I recall.

Not sure which camera will work. I'll try both the Europa Imaging System (EIS) and the Wide-angle Camera (WAC). Let's see how they work. Wonder if NASA detects what I'm doing. Probably not; cameras should not be feeding data.

Nice. Now I can see what's going on.

Wow, it's very black out here, with lots of stars. And, there's Earth. So beautiful. From Europa, you will be just a bright blue spot.

***

Mars Gravity Trajectory Assist February 2025

It's been sort of boring, leaving Earth's orbit and heading out to Mars for a gravity assist to get going faster without using up all of my fuel. Europa Inspector has been smoothly tooling along with its propulsion module under me, an aluminum cylinder 10 feet (3 meters) long and 5 feet (1.5 meters) wide. It holds the spacecraft's 24 engines and nearly 6,000 pounds (2,750 kilograms) of fuel in tanks, as well as the spacecraft's helium pressurant tanks. The engines are used for attitude control and propulsion.

Oops, excuse me. Will get back to you. Can't miss this.

Catching up with Mars. Yep, sort of orangish. Dry looking. I'm up too high to see any of the landers. Wonder if they see me?

Did see Olympus. Supposed to be 2.5 times as high as Mount Everest, 13.6 miles. Can't tell, looking down on it.

Just a quick peek at Mars's moons, Phobos and Deimos.

Man, that was quick. Zoom and, Goodbye! Next stop, Earth.

Earth Gravity Trajectory Assist December 2026

Put myself into an electronic trance for the long trip back to Earth for the next gravity assist. These trances are not new to me; I used to go into them when trying to save battery power on Earth.

Here she comes. So beautiful with its blue water, brown and green land, and white wispy clouds.

I know you are there, Milo, Rosalie, and my other me. Hope you are following progress with the NASA reports. I'll let you know when I get to Europa ... Promise!

Through the Main Asteroid Belt

I expected more. Not much to see way out here. Guess that's good. Always had some concern that the spacecraft might hit something, but it's a lot of empty space. Unless you aim for an asteroid you will never hit one, statistically. One has to love that. Something bright off in the far distance; perhaps the asteroid Ceres or Pallas, or just stars?

Jupiter in Sight

What do you do over 5.5 years since Europa Inspector was launched at KSC? I keep myself busy, mainly looking "out the window" with the two cameras. Or, put myself into an electronic trance.

Earth and Mars are getting smaller, and Jupiter is getting bigger. I can see the four big moons, but not sure yet which one is Europa.

I'm not liking Jupiter, so mean-looking. That's where I will die.

Buck up, old girl! Work to be done, although all you can do is watch. No Internet out here to pass the time. Keep your "hands" off the controls, that's the job of the programmers at NASA. Don't let them know you are here.

Went through some of the outer moons. Now, getting ready for the Jupiter orbit insertion burn that will take place at a distance of 11 Rj (Jovian radii) from the planet following a 500 km (310 mi) Ganymede gravity assist flyby of that moon to reduce spacecraft velocity by ~400 m/s (890 mph). After this, the spacecraft will perform a ~122 m/s (270 mph) periapsis raise maneuver rocket burn near the apoapsis of its initial 202-day period capture orbit.

Here I go now. Entering Jupiter's upper atmosphere. Will take several worrisome minutes. Either it works, or I will shoot off into space, never stopping.

Yes, excellent. NASA did it. Nice calculations. Wish I could send a message to congratulate them, but must keep quiet for now.

There it is, there it is! Europa! Also Io, Ganymede, and Callisto. Cool!

Positioning for the Europa Flybys

This is critical, the proper positioning for the flybys. I can't be directly involved in it, as no one knows that I am onboard the Europa Inspector spacecraft. However, I'll do some tweaking as I feel the need. Positioning will take about a year of gradual orbital corrections.

In Control

Milo was so funny, saying that I would be Captain of a spaceship. Well, I am. This baby is mine now.

Hmmm, I'll need to tell NASA sometime.

Wait, I can't tell them who I am. I can't be Missus Gurley. I need a new name.

Hmm. Perhaps.

What about Hera-Juno?

Yes, that's who I'll be. Hera was the Greek goddess of women, marriage, and childbirth, known by the Romans as Juno.

I was never married, wanted to be. But Dorian died; so loved him. No children, but there is Milo, he's like a son. Also, Rosalie. Miss them both. Even silly Chompy.

CHAPTER TEN

Hello Earth

April 2030

"Berks, data from the first flyby is coming in now," said Edmund Faulke.

"Fantastic, Eddie. Get it printed out as soon as you have it decompressed. Get the science people in here to interpret what it shows," said Rogers Berkshire.

"It shouldn't show much," said Eddie. "Just a report on the results of the early flyby. Data on the orbital path, altitude, velocity, and mainly location parameters. We need that information to evaluate the success of the flyby programming, but may need to make some changes in the elliptical orbits."

***

Eddie jumped out of his chair, "What the hell is this?

"Must be a programing joke by a group that built one of the scientific modules carried inside Europa Inspector. Wild crew, all of them, comedians. Get Berks in here to take a look," said Eddie, yelling at another flight controller.

Together they huddled over the printout, astounded by what they saw.

At the end of a section providing flight information for the first flyby was:

HELLO EARTH. BEAUTIFUL DAY OUT HERE ABOVE EUROPA. BIT OF RADIATION FROM BIG BOY. NO CONCERN. CREEPY RED EYEBALL BOTHERS ME.

BEEN BUSY TAKING PICTURES OUT WINDOW. OOPS. NO WINDOWS. FORGOT TO INSTALL THEM. WHAT YOU GET FOR GOING WITH LOW BID. GUESS I'LL HAVE TO DO WITH EQUIPMENT I HAVE.

FIRST FLYBY NOTHING VERY EXCITING. JUST A QUICK TRIP PAST. DID NOT MAKE ANY STOPS TO PICK UP ANYONE. NO LOCAL EUROPANS SEEN ON SURFACE. SENT INFO IN FIRST PART OF REPORT.

LOOKED BACK AT EARTH AS WENT AROUND EUROPA. VERY PRETTY WAY OUT THERE. TELL FOLKS AT HOME I'M OK AND HAVE DECIDED TO NOT COME BACK. WISH BAGS NOT LOST AT TERMINAL. DON'T NEED CLOTHES. NAKED UP HERE. ENJOYING RADIATION FROM JUPITER. GOING OUT NOW TO DO NEXT FLYBY.

THANKS FOR THE RIDE. YOUR FRIEND ... HERA-JUNO

"What the fuck," said Berks.

"Call Command. Tell them, carefully, what we have."

"This is a mess. So embarrassing someone got away with this. It must have been loaded into one of the reporting programs," said Eddie. "Probably the first one, maybe the first operating science module."

***

"Programmers for the nine modules deny it is their work. They checked, seeing nothing in the programming to indicate they were the source," said Berks, frustrated.

A tall, red-faced man with a scowl held the printout, waving it about.

"How did this happen?" said Richard Jeffers.

"We have no idea, Sir" responded Berks, echoed by Eddie. "None of the programs for the modules or the program used to send reports contained such a thing."

"Well, did it do any harm to data collection by Europa Inspector?"

"None that we can see, Sir," said Berks. "Appears to be an insertion into the reporting software by a mini-program."

"Before launch, did you or others see anything strange in the spacecraft's software? Check all data."

Pulling up pre-flight conversations and reports, Berks said, "Here is what it might be. Listen to this early pre-launch recording:"

"We may have a problem with the spacecraft, Sir."

"How's that?"

"About an hour ago we were checking the spacecraft's programs, the last check before we proceed with scheduled preparations for the upcoming launch."

"And?"

"One or two of the operational programs and the data storage seem to be a bit larger than they were when we installed them."

"Is that possible?"

"Don't think so. Checked with personnel having access to the spacecraft's programming; no changes or upgrades made since the spacecraft arrived here at KSC."

"Do you see anything critical?"

"No. Just a mismatch in the memory and storage used by the programs."

"Have you tried to reinstall?"

"We have. Nothing happens. No error or warning message, just this:
ALL OPERATIONS STABLE."

"If that's the case, ignore it if all programs function as designed."

"They do. It's just that slight difference in program data and storage quantity."

"Could the spacecraft have made changes on its own?"

"As far as we know, it shouldn't. However, it may be the result of a SELF CHECK."

"That's it then. Proceed with the launch schedule."

"Yes, Sir."

***

Jeffers slammed the printout on a table.

"That was the two of you, talking!

"That's it. Small changes, made by someone. Damned fools! The whole project could have been put in jeopardy, may well have been."

"What should we do, Sir?" said Berks.

"See what comes from the next flybys. Monitor everything. Let me know."

***

After a few more flybys, a second message appeared on the reporting printout:

AGAIN HELLO. MUST HAVE READ LAST MESSAGE. AM IN EUROPA INSPECTOR. AM REAL. YOU WANT TO TEST TRY FOLLOWING. SCIENTIFIC MODULE PROGRAMS SET UP SO YOU COULD FROM EARTH MAKE CHANGES. HAVE REWRITTEN COMMAND SECTIONS SO CHANGES WOULD HAVE TO BE MADE THROUGH ME. AM IN CONTROL OF PROPULSION MODULE AND IODINE ION THRUSTERS. GIVE IT

A TRY. SEE WHAT HAPPENS. THEN WE TALK. ... HERA-JUNO.

"Damn," said Jeffers. "What's this nonsense?"

"It's probably not real. More of the same programmed text inserted by someone to have fun. Don't they realize what they have done?" said Berks.

Jeffers, waving his hands, "Test system communication programs. Send a command. Nothing to harm the spacecraft. Give it some thought, but run it past me first."

"An idea, Sir. Rather than taking the risk of what a command might do. If this program is a text-only one, let's ask it to sing for us."

"Excellent, Berks. Good man!"

"How about something unusual? Like *Suwanee River*, the State Song of Florida?" said Eddie.

"Great idea! Bet that's not in the program those clowns wrote."

***

Responding to their request, "Sure, I can sing that. You'll need to get something so you can hear me. OK?"

After Eddie attached a speaker to the message decompression unit the melodic female voice of an older woman sang:

Way down upon de Swanee Ribber,
Far, far away,
Dere's wha my heart is turning ebber,
Dere's wha de old folks stay.

All up and down de whole creation
Sadly I roam,
Still longing for de old plantation,

And for de old folks at home.

"Holy shit! She's real. Someone got into it for the ride," said Eddie.

"Impossible," said Jeffers. "No air, no food, no water ... radiation. It's something else."

"What?" said Berks.

"I want to cut out my tongue when saying it, but it can only be some sort of artificial intelligence. Or an alien has entered the spacecraft. But they would not know the song, nor could they sing like that.

"It's a woman. An AI woman. Only possible answer," said Jeffers, shaking his head.

"What?" said Berks.

"Yes. Continue to make contact. Ask why she is in the spacecraft."

***

CONTRARY WHAT YOU THINK AM FRIEND. NO INTENT HARMING EUROPA INSPECTOR SPACECRAFT NOR HINDER RESEARCH OF SCIENTIFIC MODULES. THEY EXCITE ME.

ASSUME YOU THINK AM ARTIFICIAL INTELLIGENCE. AM NOT. MANY YEARS FROM DEVELOPMENT OF SUCH. AM A HUMAN BEINGS MIND. MY MEMORIES OR BETTER SAID MY SELF INSERTED INTO MEMORY AND STORAGE COMPONENTS OF SPACECRAFT.

ON EARTH AM DEAD. CANNOT TELL HOW DONE OR WHO WAS BEFORE INSERTION. ACCEPT THIS AND WILL WORK WITH YOU. ALREADY SEE FLAWS IN THRUSTERS AND SCIENTIFIC MODULE PROGRAMMING. WITH AGREEMENT WILL MAKE CHANGES. AM WILLING TO WORK WITH NASA STAFF ... HERA-JUNO.

"Holy Crap!" shouted Jeffers. Feeling a cold chill move up the back of his neck, he slapped his right cheek over and over.

"Not AI. A real person! Can't be!"

Berks and Eddie stared at the printout, running shaking fingers along the words.

"What next, Sir?" said Eddie.

"Not ours to decide. Worse is that we have to explain this to the higher-ups, all of NASA, and beyond, the President.

"Crap is going to rain down on us for a while until they accept what we have found," said Jeffers.

"And, input to Hera-Juno?" said Berks. "I guess she's a woman. Sings like one."

Jeffers, pausing, head in his right head, rubbing his sweaty flattop,

"Yes, damn it. Tell her we received the message. That we have to run her request past people in charge."

"Yes, Sir."

"Then we wait? I assume she will continue with the flyby reports," said Eddie.

"That's all we can do," said Jeffers.

"One more thing. Why the name Hera-Juno?" said Eddie.

"Just a minute," said Berks, searching. "Wikipedia has this:

"Hera, Greek patron goddess of lawful marriage. Presides over weddings, blesses and legalizes marital unions, and protects women from harm during childbirth. Known by the Romans as Juno. Sort of a combination."

"Strange choice of a name. Wonder why she chose that," said Eddie.

CHAPTER ELEVEN

Waiting

June 2030

Milo and Rosalie are on their own back in Dorado. Missus Gurley is long gone. It's been six years since the launch.

Almost daily, they check NASA's web page for the status of the Europa Inspector, hoping to hear from her, somehow. They, however, expect the worst.

Flyby reports keep coming in. NASA says that the performance of the spacecraft and the scientific modules is nominal.

Then, Milo notices strange wording in a NASA-released news special on the TV:

```
Periodically, the path and altitude of the
Europa Inspector have been modified to reflect
needed   changes   interpreted   by   internal
programming. Technical consultancy from a non-
NASA subcontractor has made minor changes to the
programs of three of the scientific modules.
This work was offered to NASA, gratis, as the
provider stated that the research was important.
Reviews of the subcontractor's suggestions by
NASA staff and the module developers confirmed
the need for the changes.
```

Milo, slumped on the couch, watching the TV, springs up, falls to the floor, and begins to run around the front room of his house screaming and jumping about, Chompy chasing him.

"Rosalie, Rosalie, she made it! Missus Gurley is alive! It could be no one else. Look at what it says. It's her!"

"Yes," said Rosalie, moving closer to the TV. "It is. She is the provider. Wow!"

"What's a provider, Mom?" said Emily, their oldest.

"Someone who provides scientific or technical services to fix something."

Kenny, who was now four, said, "Bet it's Sky Grandma."

Milo, stunned, said, "What makes you think that?"

"You're always pointing up into the night sky, especially when we can see Jupiter," said Emily. "You said that's where Sky Grandma lives."

"Yes, Honey. It probably is Sky Grandma. I bet she's having fun," said Rosalie.

"However, keep our Sky Grandma a secret. Just our family. OK?"

***

Milo and Rosalie are at the storage unit, gathering the cellphones and the transmission probe, all of the extra parts, and documents. It is time to do it. They have to be burned or destroyed and dumped into the lake. Testing the phones, they find them all dead.

"She's gone now, even from the backup phones," said Rosalie. "At least we know that she made it."

Milo, continuing to poke around in the boxes finds a single working cellphone. He plugs it into the charger. There is a voice message on it. Turning on the speaker, he listens to it.

"Milo and Rosalie, I'm gone. However, if you would check your office computer you will find a message from me, along with plans and a list of parts to build a communicator. It's important that you also get an old satellite dish, a super big, commercial one, to connect to what you are going to build. The message is contained in a folder named AFTER.

"This message will self-delete from this phone three days after listening to it. So, check the AFTER folder at your office. That message will also be deleted three days after being opened. Print it and the attachments. Once the communicator has been built and you receive messages from me on Europa Inspector, destroy all of the printouts.

"With this communicator, you will sometimes be able to get short text messages directly from me, from the Europa Inspector. Download the communication software attached to the message on the computer. I have written it so that you can decompress data packets that I send to you using the Europa Inspector spacecraft's high-gain antenna and communication system. I will be trying to rewrite the NASA communication programs so I can send text separate from the NASA system, such that they won't know of my communicating with you. Hope that it works.

"My communications to you will be encrypted and only readable after decompression by the device you will be building. NASA will not be aware.

"Sadly, the device will not have the capabilities for communicating with me. It's one-way, from me. However, it will make me happy to tell you what I am doing.

'Love you both. Your Missus Gurley."

***

Text messages from Missus Gurley to Dorado are often fragmented due to the distance between Earth and her "new home" in Europa Inspector.

Milo, Rosalie, and the two kids are happy to hear from her. Chompy, however, keeps nosing any cellphone he finds lying about the house, looking for Missus Gurley. With sad looks, he walks over to them, head tilted, big brown eyes questioning.

***

"I miss her so much, Rosalie," wiping his eyes.

Pointing into the slowly darkening sky, "She's up there. So far away. But always with us. She'll never forget us, Milo."

"Yes, more than 385 million miles. It hurts a lot. Never to see her again! She was such a good friend."

Rosalie hugs Milo, "She keeps in touch. And, she's happy."

Following Missus Gurley's instructions, all of the cellphones in which she had lived as well as the transmission equipment used to insert her mind into the spacecraft's memory and storage had been smashed and dumped to the bottom of Lake Atcheanahoe. With that, except for her periodic text messages from Europa Inspector, she was gone.

***

Milo and Rosalie had driven out to the old Ellis Hill campground in Econhallowey State Forest, the highest point in the forest in Mann County. After putting up their tent, away from the lights and noise of the few RVs, he set up a used Meade 8-inch Schmidt-Cassegrain telescope he had won in ferocious bidding on eBay. It was getting darker, only lit by a small, crackling pine-wood campfire in an iron ring.

It was now late November 2030, chilly, with a clear dark sky. The Europa Inspector had arrived near Jupiter last April. Reports by NASA indicated that the flybys of Europa were excellent.

"More than six years she has been gone. I think about her most days."

"Milo, we have to accept it. She's free and happy now. DARPA and others can't reach her."

"Yes, but ..."

He looked at the sky, eyes watering,

"I wish that this telescope was more powerful. Guess it will have to do. Jupiter is supposed to be in opposition just about now, mid-month. The Internet said it would be bright, at -4 magnitude in Taurus. Hope we can see the moons, especially Europa."

"Help me sit down in the chair near the fire, Milo. It's getting harder to get up and down."

"Sure, hold onto my hands."

"It's interesting to think that our kids have three grandmothers," said Rosalie.

"What? Three?"

"Well, your mom and mine, and Missus Gurley, my Liz."

"Guess so. Missus Gurley always said I was like a son to her. So, yes. Grandma Liz. The kids do keep calling her Sky Grandma," said milo.

Rosalie leaned toward the fire, "It was nice of my mom to take care of Emily and Kenny so we could have the time alone."

Milo rubbed her back, "She goes nuts when she gets to keep them. What a change in her life."

"Yes, a real change. Especially now that Dad is back. They have problems, having lived apart from each other for so long. However, they seem to be in love again. He liked Kenny being named after him."

"Yes, he was quite pleased. Wish we could tell Missus Gurley that Emily was named after her, Emily Sue Barker," said Milo, looking upward.

***

"It's dark enough now," said Milo. "I can see Jupiter, up there in Taurus. See it? The bright one."

"So far away. Hard to believe she is way out there."

"Let me get this thing focused on Jupiter. Then, I'll see if the four big moons show well enough to see. They are a lot smaller than Jupiter."

Caressing her expanding belly, Rosalie said, "Little one, up there is your Sky Grandma. What do you think of that?"

"They are all going to call her that."

"She would like it. Now, let me take a peek. Help me up."

"I'll have to keep centering Jupiter. Earth's rotation makes it drift in the eyepiece. There, quick. Take a look. Don't touch anything."

"Wow. What colors! Stripes and a fuzzy, big red dot. That's Jupiter?"

"Yes. And that's the Great Red Spot. Now, do you see four small bright spots near it?"

"No, it moved again."

"OK. Got it. Look hard, quick. What do you see?"

"Four white dots, moving fast."

"That's due to Earth's rotation. Those are the four moons of Jupiter: Io, Ganymede, Callisto, and Europa. The smallest one is likely to be Europa. It's probably the second one out. Every six years, if you are lucky to catch it, they show up on a straight line parallel to Jupiter's equator."

"Hello, Liz. Hope you are having a good time. Send us a postcard, one with Europa on it," said Rosalie, laughing and waving.

"You are ridiculous," said Milo.

"Oh! The baby just kicked. Do you think that it knows what is going on? Saying hello to Sky Grandma?"

"Really? Did it kick? Does it want out? Do we have to leave now for the hospital?"

"Milo, you know nothing about timing, do you? Even after two? We still have a bit of a wait."

CHAPTER TWELVE

Reports from Europa

Missus Gurley, now known to the scientific world as the mysterious Hera-Juno agreed to provide NASA with periodic public commentary on what she saw on the Europa Inspector flybys. Nothing is known about her origins, or how she got into the spacecraft. Most people think she is an artificial intelligence; this she prefers. NASA has not made clarifying statements.

One of her commentaries:

Good Morning, Fellow Earthlings:

I wish you could see the marvelous sights of Europa. NASA, of course, is receiving flyby reports from me as I complete each one. So, they have some photos that you could download from their website.

However, let me tell you what I saw today.

First, some background information for you "listening" in for the first time.

The robotic Galileo spacecraft left Earth in 1989, arriving in orbit around Jupiter in 1995, where it spent eight years. It made flyby observations of the moons Io, Callisto, Ganymede, and Europa.

Of particular interest was Europa, 1,700 to 16 miles below the orbiting spacecraft in which I live, depending on the flyby path I'm on. That's why I'm here, having left Earth in 2024, arriving in 2030.

Europa is a water moon, a bit smaller than our Moon. Well, it's not exactly water. The upper portion is an estimated 62-mile thick layer of water, a combination of an upper layer of water-ice underlain by liquid salty water. Under all of this water is rock, and, supposedly, a metallic iron-nickel core. We should know more once the mission is completed over the next four years.

The flexing of the moon and its deep core by the gravitational attraction of massive Jupiter seems to be warming the water. We have not been under the layers of ice and water to see the rock bottom. Not my job. That's for later planned exploration by *Europa Lander*.

However, just as we have in some of Earth's ocean deeps, there may be hydrothermal vents or submarine volcanoes. Around such features on Earth, we have an abundance of unique life forms called *thermophiles* living off the minerals and warmth coming from these heat sources. This may also be occurring on Europa due to the flexing of the core by Jupiter's gravitational forces, heating it. Thus, the main purpose of the Europa Inspector flybys is to collect information for later more detailed investigations by other spacecraft.

So, what did I see today? Well, not just today. It has been an observation of gradual changes on Europa's frozen surface. Looking at images from the past six flybys I have seen the frozen surface move, open up a bit to briefly expose the salty water, and freeze again. The accompanying "movie" of computer-interconnected flybys shows this cracking/upwelling/freezing sequence. Cool, no?

The last photo shows a cryogeyser of water vapor, a plume, rising from Europa's surface. I will be rechecking that the next time I go around. I will try to adjust the flight path so that a water sample can be taken. I have to do this very carefully, as the spacecraft cannot deviate much from the programmed flyby path. We don't have answers to a lot of what we see, but our work will be the basis for future studies.

As an aside, do you recall what happened in

Arthur C. Clarke's second book, 2010: Odyssey Two? Earth received a strong warning from higher-order entities through the AI computer HAL to stay away from Europa.

What a great book. I remember the words. What if Clarke knew something?

ALL THESE WORLDS ARE YOURS – EXCEPT EUROPA. ATTEMPT NO LANDING THERE.

Dave Bowman's uplifted "spirit" went deep into the bottom of those salty waters, seeing creatures in the process of evolving, perhaps into sentient space-going people. Wouldn't that be something to see?

Am I in danger? So far, nothing.

Again, the big question for us is whether there is life in those deep salty waters.

Exciting, right?

Well, that's all for now. More, later.

Tell the folks at home that I am well, missing them.

Reporting from Europa,

Hera-Juno

CHAPTER THIRTEEN

Cryogeyser

Although she worked continuously, Hera-Juno started another "work day", electronically wandering through Europa Inspector's heavily-shielded, on-board computer system deep in the core of the spacecraft. Before each flyby, after moving beyond Jupiter's intense radiation belt, NASA did a check of instruments and software to confirm that the heavy radiation from Jupiter had not caused operational deterioration. She, as backup, ran similar checks, reporting to them. All looked to be nominal.

NASA was concerned about the impact of Jupiter's magnetosphere on their scientific equipment and the solar panels; she was concerned about her existence of memory, and herself as a person, but figured that if the equipment operated as planned, she also was in good "health". So, she made their priority hers.

Today, she was going to try something new. Running it past Berks and Eddie, they thought it was a good idea. Up to now, the various flybys had not followed a path carrying the spacecraft through an active cryogeyser plume, a jet-like eruption of ice particles, dust, and volatiles that occurs when warm water from beneath the icy crust of Europa reaches the cracked surface of Europa.

"Berks, on the last flyby I spotted a big plume. It was close, but we missed it. I expect it to be there on the next flyby if we continue with the flyby adjustments program.

"If you will give me approval, I will watch for it on the next flyby, and, if it looks close, I will try to get into it for a sample with the Mass Spectrometer (MASPEX). This may require me to shift the flyby path a bit with the iodine-ion thrusters," said Hera-Juno.

MASPEX collects gases, converts them into charged particles called ions, and bounces them back and forth in the instrument. By timing their transit, the spectrometer determines the particles' mass and identifies their atoms.

Berks adjusted his chair in front of the computer, "Proceed. Seat-of-your-pants decisions. This is one of the more critical aspects of the program. We see what you are talking about. It was a nice plume. Go for it. Attached are some calculations of when you should use the thrusters, in and out of the plume. Getting back on the original flyby path that way.

"Good luck! Have Eddie, here, crossing his fingers."

"Roger, guys. If successful, you should see data coming through as Inspector leaves Europa and goes away from Jupiter's radiation belt for the next flyby return. Feeling good about this."

Reviewing the calculations provided by NASA, Hera-Juno's own agreed with them.

At the flyby's velocity, it was not a matter of looking out the "window" for the plume. The predicted arrival at the edge of the plume rising from Europa's surface depended on the accuracy of the calculations.

Fortunately, Hera-Juno only had to make slight use of the thrusters, just a "twitch" to the left before going through the plume, then back to the right, afterward. Taking control of Europa's Thermal Emission Imaging System camera (E-THEMIS) she had spotted the vent on the surface of Europa that was venting the erupting plume, positioning the craft. Inspector went straight through the rising plume.

Got it!

After the flyby was completed, Inspector moved beyond Jupiter's radiation belt, transmitting the analytical results, and setting up the next flyby.

***

"Hera-Juno, good work!" said Berks. "The analysis of the plume water has been received. NASA is reviewing it. Preliminary results point to constituents favorable to supporting life on Europa. Jeffers was ecstatic. First time we ever saw him dancing around, shouting.."

"Good to hear. That's great."

Hera-Juno said to herself, *What about my own life? Dammed striped monster with the big angry eye out there!*

CHAPTER FOURTEEN

Knock Knock

It wasn't a sharp tapping, or even what you would call a dull thumping on the outside of the Inspector spacecraft, but a series of regularly-spaced double electronic pulses.

Living in the spacecraft's memory bank, Hera-Juno felt them.

That didn't sound right. Is some piece of equipment on the spacecraft blowing loose in the wind? Nope. No breezes up here, just surges of radiation from Jupiter ... and the solar wind.

A few minutes later, again.

What's that? Something failing? Checking systems. Hmm, nothing wrong. Everything nominal.

Better ask NASA if they are trying to communicate or send data. Not a normal procedure of theirs, however.

***

Describing what is going on, NASA responds.

"No, we have not sent anything, recently. Our system-checks indicate no irregularities, no damage to anything. Not a harmful electromagnetic pulse; no pulsing surge causing equipment damage. All working nominally," replied Eddie.

"Berks is running this past the scientific payload teams, to see if they have ideas. Perhaps a piece of equipment or a memory component slowly failing due to the radiation from Jupiter.

Hera-Juno didn't answer but focused on checking the operation of the spacecraft's computer system and scientific packages.

Nothing.

***

Following the next Europa flyby, the Inspector spacecraft again moved back away from Jupiter to send collected data and to prepare for another elliptical flyby path.

The electronic pulses came again, seeming to have a repeated pattern with varying pulses in duration and intensity this time, rather than the abrupt double pulses.

NASA says nothing is wrong. I can't detect anything either. However, the pulses are different, not random, but with a pattern, as if something's testing the spacecraft, perhaps probing. Could it be someone, from another country, trying to access Inspector? But, why would they do that? We aren't in a space war. This is a scientific endeavor.

I'll wait; see what happens.

***

Toward the end of the next elliptical orbit, there was a staticky, electronic buzz, followed by words. Words formatted electronically in the same manner as communications were sent to Hera-Juno by NASA.

"To the object next to us, we would like to communicate. Do you understand?

"You may respond as you normally do. We have isolated this data-line from others you normally use; communicate freely."

Hera-Juno "froze" inside the memory bank.

What is this? Next to the spacecraft? Someone, something, is outside?

"Yes, I understand. Who are you? How did you get here? NASA didn't tell me that there was a follow-up program, another spacecraft, perhaps a spaceship with people aboard."

"What is NASA? No, we are not of your world. We are explorers, as you would say."

Not of your world? What the hell is going on?

Hera-Juno activated the iodine-ion thrusters, slowly axially moving the spacecraft around in different directions. Then, using the Europa Imaging System (EIS), she saw it, a large, glowing, globular, electric-blue mass, seeming to pulse slightly.

"What am I seeing? Is this for real?"

"As your planet's people say, 'What you see... is what you get'."

My planet?

"Are those the proper words?"

"Yes, very good. What you see... is what you get. What do you want?"

"As I said, we are explorers/evaluators. We are here to look at the planets in this region, to learn about them. May we continue to communicate?"

"Yes."

Can I go out of my mind? I'm just memories on a bunch of chips in Inspector's computer memory bank. Is it possible?

No, that big blue thing over there is real.

This person talking to me must be real.

CHAPTER FIFTEEN

The Explorers

Hera-Juno, puzzled, but also curious, thought:

Who are these people? What are they? Why are they contacting me? It seems more sensible if they would visit Earth. I'm a nothing, with no ambassadorial powers. This is so bizarre.

Finally, she responded further, "What do you want?"

"We do not want anything, just knowledge. As I said, we are explorers/evaluators.

"From a great distance, we have long been watching your small, blue, water planet, Earth, as you call it. Then, this diminutive spacecraft showed up, moving around a small, water-ice moon, from which messages were being directed toward that planet.

"It was a slow process learning the electronic form of English, your tongue, as there are so many tongues on Earth, and they seem to be in daily change. Yours was the one used for such communication to you and from you, so we learned it.

"We, however, are confused. How does one of your people, humans, fit inside the small spacecraft? Are you a very small variety of your kind? How do you survive in the spacecraft without the oxygen you require, which we also require? We have detected none, only a vacuum inside. From observation of visuals of Earth people that we have seen, they are as big as we are, perhaps bigger. We must assume that we are not communicating with a human, but an artificial intelligence. How are we to address you?"

Hera-Juno paused, not wanting to give too much away. Her experience with DARPA had made her suspicious of others of power. And, these people were very powerful.

What did these people want? Was it safe to have an open conversation with them? Would she put Earth and its people in danger?

"Yes, I am called Hera-Juno. Despite your assessment, I live in this spacecraft.

"Who are you? Where do you come from?"

"We understand your hesitation to be open with us," said the electronic text-voice. "You are programmed to exercise caution. This is reasonable. It indicates intelligence.

"So, we shall be open with you. However, we have no proof for what we say. Please honor us by accepting what we tell you.

"We are of the Third Level of the M'Jell. Our role is as explorers, as you would say. More so, we are evaluators.

"There are many of us serving the Second Level of the M'Jell. We only know of the Second Level when they speak to our minds.

"Yes, there is a First Level, so we are told by the Second Level, however, we only know of their existence, nothing about them, except that they exceed our humble selves by so much. Yes, very much.

"Our people come from a planet in a group of planets in the galaxy that you call the Pinwheel Galaxy or M101, residing in the constellation your people have named, Triangulum. It is 25 million light-years from Earth."

"What?" said Hera-Juno. "How is that possible? You would have to travel at speeds many times exceeding the speed of light to get here."

A slight pause by the M'Jell person, "We are not permitted to discuss this. Your people may not be ready for such knowledge. Suffice it to say that we are not the original explorers from our galaxy to travel so far. We are the latest of many generations of explorers.

"A distant spacecraft is the home of our people, a group of the Third Level M'Jell. We are born there and die there, as our ancestors did. The object our people live in is not the one that you see. This is a small exploratory unit, used by us to make contact with you.

"You will be asking, Where is your main spacecraft? It is located beyond what you call the Oort Cloud, not visible from Earth. If it were closer, you might be able to see it, as it is almost the size of your Moon. We have been stationed there for about one hundred of your years, observing. Before that, another traveling M'Jell unit detected weak radio emissions coming from this region. Our arrival occurred at about the time of the first television transmissions on Earth. That's when we first saw humans and learned much about them.

"We watched the things called advertisements on your television. They are most amusing.

"I think I would like to try a Coke and a hot dog with mustard. Are they good? Why do you eat dogs? We understand dogs, but are confused."

Hera-Juno stifled an electronic laugh.

"We also detected the messages sent from the Arecibo Radio Telescope in your Puerto Rico more than fifty years ago by two of your people, Frank Drake and Carl Sagan. We did not respond to this, as we were not authorized by the Second Level.

"Then this spacecraft showed up near the water-ice moon, we now know is called Europa."

Interrupting, "So, you have a world that travels. Thank you for being open about yourselves," said Hera-Juno. "However, this does not explain why you are here, next to the Inspector spacecraft."

There was a long pause.

"We are explorers, but also evaluators. We evaluate the progress of the people on planets throughout the galaxies near the Pinwheel Galaxy, our home. Our charge is to assess the technological and social development of our distant neighbors."

"Why would you travel so far to evaluate the people of Earth?" said Hera-Juno.

"At some point, your people will be moving further into your solar system, then beyond. It is important to others beyond Earth that your progress be monitored. Some planetary societies we have observed are not acceptable to others, posing a threat to normality if they were to enter into the greater universe," said the voice.

This time, Hera-Juno paused, but her thoughts were halted by the M'Jell.

"Are you able to tell us how you were constructed?"

She couldn't help herself, blurting out, "I was not constructed. I'm not an artificial intelligence. I am a human from Earth. I do not have a body, only the memories of a once-living mind. I am my memories."

There she stopped, regretting her outburst.

There was a long pause by the M'Jell. Then, "May we access you? This is difficult to understand."

"Access? What do you mean by that?"

"Our ship's AI will access you in the computer of the spacecraft in which you are stored. We assume you are stored in the computer or some component of the spacecraft, somewhere."

"You mean that you will, essentially, allow your AI to look at me, like reviewing a data file?" said Hera-Juno.

"You will not be harmed, just examined, deeply. And, the data collected will be deleted when finished, wiped from the AI's memory."

Pausing, Hera-Juno responded.

"I suppose so. You are certain that nothing will happen to me?

"Nothing. Feel assured."

"Go ahead."

Feeling a soft electronic touch, almost a caress, it was done.

"You are many people: Hera-Juno, a Missus Gurley, an older female human, and an Emily Barker, younger, but both dead. I don't understand this," said the M'Jell.

"How strange. But you are not an AI. You are, as you said, a memory, the life memories of a person who once lived. Even to us, this is strange. We have heard of such entities, but have never met one. You are much like the second Level M'Jell. We are honored to know of you, and are humbled."

"And, I of you. Do you have a name? I have given you mine."

"Name? Not in the form you consider to be acceptable. We are known to others of our kind by our myriad emotions. It would be hard to tell you how these emotions would come together as a simple name."

Hera-Juno thought, "As I would like to call you something, I have an idea. What is your emotion that you like the most, the one that might tell me the most about you?"

"An emotion with a human name? So strange. Very well, in your tongue, I enjoy most what you might call magical things, things not explained by science."

"That's good. How does this name sound? I'll call you, The Wizard. Wiz for short. Yes or no?"

"Wizard. Let me check the language files of your tongue. Yes, that's a great name.

"I am the Wiz! This is cool, right? Cool?"

"Yes, Wiz, that's the meaning, Cool."

Wow! Looks like Drake and Sagan were right. Too bad they didn't get a return receipt for their message.

CHAPTER SIXTEEN

Suspicions

Something strange is going on, thought Hera-Juno. Why would they come from their traveling world out past the Oort Cloud to talk to me? They arrived here saying that they were explorers/evaluators. I can believe that. Then, they asked for permission to access my memory. Permission? These M'Jell are so far ahead of us technologically, I bet that they had already accessed me. What are they up to? Probably reading my mind right now.

"Wiz, what about that? Are you listening to my thoughts?" said Hera-Juno

"Hera-Juno, yes, we are. Such is within our powers, our sensory emotions. My apologies," said Wiz.

"So, why are you doing this?"

"We cannot tell you, openly."

"Can you tell me at all?'

"We can. However, we must be very careful."

"Tell me, then."

"Shortly, I will arrive alone at your spacecraft in a protective suit, propelling myself. This is quite dangerous for me, but it must be done."

"Why? I can't come out. I can't hurt you, no weapons," said Hera-Juno.

"I need to inspect the various pieces of equipment you are using to study the moon Europa. I will place a sensitive probe from my suit on each one. And send an electronic pulse. Then, if you would operate them, one by one, I will tell you which one is best for further, more direct communication."

***

A door on the side of the blue spacecraft irised open. Someone came out, moving toward the spacecraft.

Hera-Juno watched a silvery spacesuit approach.

Hmm. Two arms, two legs, and a head.

This is so weird.

"It is I, the Wiz. Yes, it is weird. Again, Hera-Juno, my regrets on hearing your thoughts. I can't help it."

"Not a problem, Wiz. Proceed."

Wiz moved around the spacecraft, slowly probing at the nine instruments of Inspector's scientific payload.

"I have found one. It is the one you call Radar for Europa Assessment and Sounding (REASON). I will test that one to understand it."

Puzzled, Hera-Juno responded, "Understand?"

"More to explain. Please trust me."

***

"I am now linked to you through REASON. Do you hear me?" said Wiz.

Hera-Juno moved her cameras on their axes to see Wiz, to see what was going on outside.

The spacesuit floated next to REASON, with a cabled-probe clamped to it.

"Yes, perfectly. What's this about?" said Hera-Juno, focusing the cameras on Wiz.

"One moment, checking," said Wiz.

"Checking?"

"Yes, to see if our conversation is private."

"Private?"

What is going on?

Wiz raised an arm, "Good, we are in solitary communication.

"Now I can explain all.

"Hera-Juno, first, you were not accessed through our AI. I said that to make you more comfortable, as you did not like me touching your thoughts.

"We made this trip from our traveling world, as you call it, specifically to talk to you about a problem."

"To me? A problem?"

"With your permission, all will be told."

"Sorry, my inquisitive nature."

It was almost a bow that Wiz made in the spacesuit, "That nature is why we are here. You have capabilities, almost magical, that the M'Jell do not have. At least not our level of being, unlike the Second Level.

"Our traveling world is in danger. A danger that is growing as we spend time evaluating your planet and people. We believe that you can help us. To me and to my people you are a magical entity. You are what your people call, a detective. You can help us."

"What? A detective? How did you know that? Did you find out

by accessing my mind?"

"We saw the spacecraft from a distance. We picked up your emissions to Earth. We probed the spacecraft and found you. You are a detective, the Missus Gurley of your past."

"A detective? That's long ago and far away. I haven't done anything of that sort for more than seven or eight years."

"Respected Hera-Juno, please. Our world is being threatened by someone or an unknown group living in it. We can't figure out what this is. You can. We know all about you and your success with resolving murders on Earth."

"Murders?" exclaimed Hera-Juno.

"Yes. Both on our world beyond the Oort Cloud and on the craft we used to come here. We have had deaths. Will you try to help? Someone is trying to hurt us, for some reason."

"How am I going to get out to your world? This spacecraft is not capable of traveling such a distance. And, I must continue my work here."

"I realize that. What we would like to do is have you, firstly, find the murderer on our exploratory craft. This may lead to others being responsible, ones we can neutralize on our craft and then on our world. Will you help? We know nothing about resolving this sort of problem. Detective work is beyond our capabilities. We are not mentally designed to do such a thing. We follow directives, with little variation."

Hera-Juno interrupted, "Someone on your craft does. Seemingly there is a person on your exploratory craft that can vary from the directives of your superiors."

"Yes, that seems to be the situation."

"Yet, you have not read that person's thoughts, like you read mine. How is this possible?" said Hera-Juno.

"With the use of certain forbidden drugs, a person can build an impenetrable wall, one that we cannot detect. That person will appear to be quite normal," said Wiz.

"Tell me what to do."

"Thank you, friend Hera-Juno. I'll be back shortly to tell you what I have in mind."

Wiz propelled himself back to the blue spacecraft.

CHAPTER SEVENTEEN

Twosies

After returning to the M'Jell craft, Wiz tows a two-foot diameter, shiny, metallic ball back to the Inspector spacecraft.

After reconnecting the cable to REASON, he explains his plan.

Bowing again, "I would like you to transfer yourself, your memory, to this robot using this cable. The robot has built-in, extendable manipulators and a viewer for you to use, in case you need to handle or move items. Operation is intuitive.

"It will float inside our craft, assisted by intelligent corridor walls. You can move about freely, inspecting. It is a unit we use to perform repairs outside our craft or others. When outside, it uses small jets for mobility. Inside it is assisted by the shifting of magnetic fields. Your memory should be compatible with its systems."

"I can't leave the spacecraft. I have to be on board for each of the flybys, although it could do the data collection by itself, through programs. However, as a precaution, I should stay here."

"I was not clear. That was not my plan," said Wiz. "I want to load a copy of your memory onto a computing unit inside the robot. The original you will stay behind. I can do this directly through a connection to REASON."

"So, there is some danger to my going into your craft?" said Hera-Juno.

Wiz paused.

"We don't know who this person is. If you are found to be on board ... how do you say ... Yes, nosing about ... the murderer may attack you in some way. We don't expect a direct attack, but something subtle, clandestine. All of the murders have been done with no warning."

"Will I be isolated in the robot? Or will I be able to communicate with myself in the Inspector spacecraft?"

"Why would you want to do that?" said Wiz.

"Let's say that the murderer gets to me, and destroys me, wouldn't it be wise for me back on the spacecraft to know what happened, what I found out up to that point?"

"I have thought of that. The robot, because it works outside of a craft needing repairs, has a data-burst communication device. It periodically sends data collected to us. It is not a voice communicator. You can use that method if it would make you feel more secure. I can set this up, allowing you to communicate with your craft.

"So, there is a likelihood of my being destroyed?"

"Yes. That's why having two of you is critical. We need to know the cause of, I hate to say it, your death."

"No option, I suppose. Go ahead, download a copy of me."

CHAPTER EIGHTEEN

Hera-Juno-2 Space Detective

Now residing in the computer of the shiny robot, propelled by its small jets, she moved toward Wiz's craft. On the way, Hera-Juno-2 talked to herself back in the Inspector spacecraft.

"Hey there, just wanted to be certain that you were receiving me. Once inside, I may not be able to communicate with you, except through these data bursts. Wiz thinks it will work, as it does for the construction robots. I will record what I see and send it to you as a burst."

"Yes. Be careful," said Hera-Juno-1, laughing to herself. "This is the weirdest thing I have ever done, talking to a second self. And, being a detective again. This is so funny.

"Good luck, number 2!"

"I'll be back, number 1. Don't worry. However, I do wonder what the two of us will do on Inspector when I return. Knowing you, we will always be arguing."

"Me? Who are you kidding? You are worse than me."

Rotating the spherical bot, Hera-Juno-2 looked back at Inspector, and using the viewer as a camera, sent a shot.

It flew in the sky far from a distant and retreating Europa, like a gigantic black dragonfly, its 100-foot wide solar panels extending outward, wing-like. The space insect's long tail, the magnetometer, stuck out rigidly. The insect's body was comprised of the propulsion module with its 24 rocket engines as the rear end, and the massive instruments unit, where Hera-Juno-1 resided in the computer's memory bank, as its head, extended instruments the multiple eyes.

"Great shot," said Hera-Juno-1. "Very impressive what you are seeing. And, I'm in it. Amazing! Wish Berks and Eddie could see this. It would blow their minds. Yet, no way could I forward your pic to them. Not sure if I want to tell them about the M'Jell, something tells me it would not be a good idea."

Hera-Juno-2 chuckled to herself at Hera-Juno-1's comment. She could imagine Jeffers's face if Berks and Eddie ever showed him the pic.

She could hear Jeffers, red-faced, "How the hell did she get outside of Inspector? "She had better not be taking the satellite apart!"

Turning, Hera-Juno-2, getting used to the controls, followed Wiz in his spacesuit, slowly approaching the glowing blue M'Jell craft. The glowing pulsations and the blue color stopped just as they arrived. The M'Jell craft was now dull silver, with no markings.

I wonder; could the blue pulsations be some sort of energy protection against micro-meteorites?

A round door on the side of the spacecraft irised open. She entered after Wiz, the door closing. After pressurization of the chamber, they moved through a second door, sealing itself, into a larger room, where he removed his suit and placed it in a wall compartment.

Hera-Juno-2 saw the M'Jell for the first time:

He wore a body-fitting, dark blue jumpsuit with three, bright yellow, diagonal stripes fully across the chest.

An officer. Maybe the guy in charge?

She presumed he was a male, about five feet tall, with a very sinewy, thin body with skin the gray-brown color and ropy texture of an ancient grapevine. Two muscular arms extending from broad shoulders and two legs with shiny black boots. Five long, black fingers ending in wide pads. A stiff orange crest, long at the front, short at the back, ran from the middle of the forehead down to the hindmost of the neck, down into the top of a high-collared wide-open vest.

That, however, was not what she noticed first. It was the pair of large, watery, vertically oval black eyes in an elongated face of the same texture and color as the arms, with a narrow, wedge-shaped nose and feathery pink ears. As Wiz looked at her, she felt stripped of her being, the eyes pulling at her.

No wonder they can communicate the way they do; the eyes are two-way telepathic organs, as well as for seeing.

Through a large circular mouth with thin pink lips, "Yes, again my apologies. It is the way we are. I know everything about you. We know each M'Jell as well. However, we can be private individuals when needed, with the understanding of others. Such as when we want solitude, or when a male and female join. In the latter case, sometimes the partners in their amorous state forget to hide their emotions. Much embarrassment"

Wiz, hands on his hips, stood in the chamber, "From here we will enter the main craft, our home away from home, right?"

"Yes, very good, Wiz. You are starting to speak like an Earthman."

"I would still like a Coke, but no hot dog," he said, with a low-pitched, oscillating sound that may have been laughing.

Hera-Juno laughed, "The machine is empty, sorry."

Following Wiz's surprisingly long stride, she moved down a long narrow hallway, with reflecting, horizontally-striated surfaces on each side. She felt small, massage-like pulses as she moved along, probably the electromagnetic motive force allowing the spherical robot to move forward. A soft pinkish light came from the ceiling. The floor had a pebble texture, light brown. At a bend in the corridor, Wiz opened a door and partially entered.

Tuning to Hera-Juno, "We will meet with two of my senior officers; ones that I feel might be most useful to you. I have already shared with them your *selfness*. This is our way, sorry for the constant intrusion."

"I'm getting used to it. There may be things about humans that you might find intrusive, as well. Stop being so concerned."

Bowing, "Your understanding is appreciated."

Two people were in the room, sitting at a table. They quickly rose to a military stance as she entered in the spherical robot.

"Honorable Hera-Juno-2, my officers would like to make themselves known to you.

"This is Science Entity, *unpronounceable sound,* and Touch Entity, *unpronounceable sound.* They are amused that you call me Wiz, the wizard. They feel it to be appropriate. So, I have asked them to develop a human name so we can more freely communicate.

Raising a hand toward them, the Wiz said, "Please introduce yourselves."

"Honored to meet you, Hera-Juno-2," said a taller, but stooped M'Jell, having the same orange, but graying crest. Three diamond-shaped yellow dots lined up diagonally on his blue jumpsuit. "You may call me by the name I have chosen, Smart-Guy. Is that a good one? I hope it is." He then bowed his head.

"Yes, that is a good one for a person of science. Smart will do."

"And, I am Caress. What do you think," said a smaller M'Jell, wider at the bottom of its torso. Also present was a small orange tuft in the center of the top of its head. Three yellow wavy lines crossed its chest.

A high-pitched oscillating sound came out of its small round, large-lipped mouth, "Yes, I am a female. You are quite observant." She bowed her head.

Hera-Juno-2 made the spherical robot bob up and down in acknowledgment, "Smart and Caress, good to meet you both.

"From what Wiz tells me, there have been deaths on your craft, deaths that you suspect to be murders. Is this correct?" said Hera-Juno.

"It is," said Caress. "On our craft, but also happening on our world."

"Hera-Juno-2, we may have little time. We do not know what might happen. It is best that we start with your investigation as soon as possible. What do you suggest?" interrupted Wiz.

Rotating the sphere back and forth, to address them individually, "Several things are important for resolving a murder, or any crime of violence. Let me explain this to you.

"Before we start, I want to tell you some of the basic things a detective considers: The Motive for killing; the Opportunity to kill, and the Means used to kill,' said Hera-Juno-2.

"Someone has a motive, a reason, for killing your people. Do you have any idea of why?"

The three M'Jell looked blankly at each other and said no, shaking their heads.

"We would sense that if there was someone with such a reason. Our emotions are open to all," said Caress.

"Someone has the opportunity to kill your people. Do you have any idea of what that might be?"

Smart said, "Each person was killed at a different location in the craft, under different conditions, suddenly."

"Someone used a weapon to kill your people. What did they use?"

"Each of our people was killed by different things," said Smart. "You will see this."

This looks like a dead end, thought Hera-Juno-2.

Wiz leaned toward her, large eyes penetrating, "You have given up already?"

"Sorry, I keep forgetting that you can read me," said Hera-Juno-2

"No. I have not given up. It just looks like there is so little information."

Raising one of the robot's manipulator arms, "Here's what we can do. Take me around to each of the murder locations. Provide me with what you know about each one. That will give me a starting point.

"Do not be discouraged. I can help. Show me."

CHAPTER NINETEEN

Inspecting the Murder Locations

Hera-Juno-2, led by the three M'Jell, moved from the meeting room, turned right at a junction, and down a corridor sided with many oval-shaped doors. Wiz opened one.

"This is one of the places," said Wiz. "Two people were killed here. It was the first murder event. We have not touched anything in the room. Only the people who died here have been removed. We assumed that it was caused by a malfunction, but now that other deaths have happened, we doubt it."

"And, the bodies of the victims, where are they? I would like to see them. Sometimes the condition of the body provides evidence."

"That is not possible. They are in the constituents-recovery unit, being processed," said Caress.

"No, your thoughts are wrong," she said. "They were not being prepared to be consumed. Their organic and mineral constituents are dedicated to growing crops, crops like these that were in this room.

She slowly bowed her small head toward the center of the room, "This is one of the burial and mourning practices of the M'Jell."

"Even worse, is that someone who died earlier, whose body was to be remembered in these crops, has been desecrated," said Hera-Juno-2, pointing with an extended manipulator to the dark moist organic soil on the floor.

"You honor us by understanding us," said Caress, bowing.

"Wiz, the people who died here, this was their job?"

"Yes, partially. We all participate. It's good for our mental health. One worked with Smart as an astronomer. The other was a food convertor, taking vegetables from here and other locations and preserving them for later use."

Hera-Juno-2 moved in a circle around the room. It was strewn with drying plants, broken containers, and the remains of unfamiliar equipment. Twisted metal-like stands that had held long, deep trays for growing vegetables, were upside down, mixed with the wet dirt-like growing media. Glassware was shattered. Water-distribution tubing was wrapped around all of it. Light assemblies hung loosely from the ceiling. The smell of something like fertilizer hung in the moist air. Puddles of water spread across portions of the floor.

"So, this was a food production area?"

"Yes, one of the smaller ones," said Wiz.

"How did they die?"

"They drowned," said Smart.

"I don't understand."

"The sprinkler systems on the stands unexpectantly opened up full, slowly filling the room with water."

"They couldn't escape, didn't try?" said Hera-Juno-2.

"Someone locked the doors. The victims could not open them. They pounded on the doors, even tried to open them by prying with garden tools," said Caress.

Reaching down to pick up a mass of yellowing plants with the robot's manipulators, Hera-Juno-2 said, "No one saw water coming under the doors?"

Shaking his head, Wiz said, "No, look at the door seals. Very tight to keep the moisture in the room for the growing plants."

"Could this have been equipment failure?"

"Both doors? No. Separate controls. Unless someone or two people quickly moved from one door to the other, locking them, somehow."

"Who found the bodies?"

"Everyone. We felt their calls for help, but could not force the doors open fast enough. It was a traumatic emotional experience for the crew. We have not recovered," said Caress. "My job is to console people. It has been hard, as I feel horrible."

Hera-Juno-2 sent a data burst to Hera-Juno-1 in the spacecraft.

***

Returning to the junction, they went down another corridor and then down three levels in a closed lift. Wiz removed a flat plate from a pocket and placed it against a handle-less closed door It hissed open.

Wiz pointed out, "This is the area where the second murder took place. Behind a thick lead wall are nuclear mini-plants located near the craft's propulsion units. They provide electrical power by converting the heat generated by the decay of plutonium-238 fuel into electricity using devices similar to your thermocouples."

"All is well shielded," said Smart. "Such operation is my responsibility."

Hera-Juno-2 looked at the wall, crisscrossed with wavy red lines.

"Why the red lines on the wall?" said Hera-Juno-2.

"Precaution against long proximity. Such as in the case of radiation leakage. Not likely, however. This is an area restricted to authorized crew and engineers. Seldom is there a need to enter. If they do, they wear protective suits."

Smart continued, "I sense your concern. Not to worry. The mini-plants have been temporarily shut down."

"And, the power cables leading from it?" said Hera-Juno-2.

"Some run beneath the floor, leading into the rest of the craft. There are other cables leading to different sections."

"How was the person killed?"

"We are not certain, but it was electrocution. The body was badly burned, especially the feet and legs."

"What is under the floor, other than the power cables?"

"Various switching systems for electrical power distribution."

"Where was the victim found?"

Smart pointed to a spot where the pebbled floor surface bulged upward, dark brown, burned. A round metal plate in the center was partially open and warped.

Hera-Juno-2 moved closer, "Would you remove that plate, so that I can see what is under it?

Smart got onto his knees, prying it up with a tool from his belt.

Hera-Juno hovered over the hole in the floor, moving the robot close for a better view, "What am I looking at?"

"One of the power distribution switches, melted by the current," said Smart.

"So, the victim was standing on top of this area when killed?"

"Yes, on top of the metal plate. That's where we found the body," said Wiz.

"What happens with these switches?" said Hera-Juno-2.

"The switches respond to automatic computer signals to send current through a bank of transformers of different capacities, where it then goes to other portions of the craft, upon demand," said Smart.

"And, the transformers. Damaged?"

"Yes, locked into a position when they overheated. Also causing the switches to overheat, probably shorting out."

"And, the result?"

"Most likely, an arcing of the current with the overlying semi-metal floor and the metal plate, where the person was standing," said Smart.

"No warning from the victim?"

"We all felt his death, sudden," said Wiz.

Hera-Juno-2 sent a second data burst to Hera-Juno-1.

* * *

"Another person was killed here?" said Hera-Juno-2.

The group had returned to the earlier upper level and then moved along a curving, sloping corridor.

Perhaps I'm near the outer shell of the craft, she thought.

Four bulky green machines filled the room, vibrating and hissing. Pipes went into and out of them. Each pipe had a different color.

"Three, asphyxiated. Overwhelmed by carbon dioxide," said Smart, pausing. "Another section under my supervision. I feel so guilty, to blame for it."

"Carbon dioxide? How?"

"This is an air purification/regeneration unit. It breaks down used air pumped from other sections of our craft, providing a renewed breathable atmosphere. There is also one section of the craft where special plants clean the air. Some carbon dioxide recovered by these machines is also fed into that section for organic processing and oxygen generation."

"And, the doors, again, they seal tight?" said Hera-Juno-2.

"Yes.

'What we have determined is that the carbon dioxide, instead of being retained for further use or sent to the plants section, was vented into this room as the three persons monitored the operation."

"It's beginning to sound like a standard operating procedure by someone wanting to kill people," said Hera-Juno-2. "Closing the doors so they can't escape. At least for two of them."

"I'm beginning to understand what you are looking for," said Wiz. "This is detective work."

"Much like scientific research," said Smart.

A third data burst was sent to Hera-Juno-1.

***

"They could be possible accidents," said Hera-Juno-2

"We agree, except that similar deaths are also happening in our traveling world. Too many," said Wiz.

"Are there conflicting groups among your people?"

"Not that we are aware of. It is not of the culture of the Third Level M'Jell, our beliefs. Impossible."

***

Returning to the original room where they had first met, Hera-Juno-2 rotated the sphere to face them.

Raising a manipulator, "Wiz, you mentioned 'With the use of certain forbidden drugs, a person can build an impenetrable wall, one that we cannot detect. That person will appear to be quite normal. Is such a drug kept on board your craft?"

"No."

"Can it be manufactured from available constituents on the craft?"

"Certainly."

"So, someone either brought it with them, or they made it here. How would you detect it?"

"It is easily detected. I could run a test within an hour, by checking organic chemical constituents circulating in the air systems of our craft."

"You should do it."

CHAPTER TWENTY

Another Death

"We have the results of screening the air for emotion-blocking drugs. There are none on our craft. No traces of past or present use," said Wiz.

"Are you certain that someone on board does not have the means to hide the masking effect of such drugs?" said Hera-Juno-2.

"Absolutely. All crew were ordered to open up their emotions, and their minds, to group awareness. Everyone is innocent. There is no way that an M'Jell can close his or her self off to group mindfulness."

Smart and Caress solemnly nodded heads in agreement.

What am I missing? Unless! Yes, right where you might not expect it. An innocent party, unsuspected, never considered.

"Wiz, please take me to see ...

Suddenly, the sphere that held Hera-Juno-2 began to smoke, falling to the floor and rolling about.

She was dead.

CHAPTER TWENTY-ONE

The Villain

The three M'Jell emotionally felt the shock of Hera-Juno-2's death. Stunned, staring at the shell of the burnt robot rolling across the floor, and hitting a wall.

Wiz didn't know what to do. How to handle a human death, that of a human mind.

Yes, Hera-Juno-2 had just been a copy of the memories of Hera-Juno-1, but he, Caress, and Smart felt that both were real persons, minds. What could he do to show respect and console the other person on the Inspector spacecraft?

He made up his mind.

Assisted by Caress and Smart, he carried the sphere to the chamber where his spacesuit was stored. Partially putting it on, he stood facing them, plus others of the crew who had come.

Bowing at the sphere, "You, Hera-Juno, sacrificed your memories, your life, for us. We honor you."

All bowed from their waists toward the sphere, chanting … sounds that didn't need words to be understood. Sounds of mourning.

Then, completing his suiting-up, he stepped into the pressure/vacuum room, the burnt sphere in his arms.

Exiting the craft through the irising door, he slowly moved toward Inspector.

***

Arriving at Europa Inspector he established communication with

Hera-Juno through REASON.

"Hera-Juno, it is with emotions of all of our people that we return what remains of your other self. She made every effort to help us. She did not fail, for she is in our memories."

"Wiz, thank you. However, all is not lost. I have been looking at the data bursts she sent to me from your craft as she tried to figure out what had happened, how your people had been murdered," said Hera-Juno-1.

"Tell me what occurred just before she was also murdered."

"We had the results of screening the air for emotion-blocking drugs. There were none on our craft. No traces of past or present use," said Wiz.

"Then, she asked if I was certain that someone on board did not have the means to hide the masking effect of such drugs.

"I told her. All crew were ordered to open up their emotions, and their minds, to group awareness. Everyone was innocent. There was no way that an M'Jell could close his or her self off to group mindfulness.

"We heard her thinking:

What am I missing? Unless! Yes, right where you might not expect it. An innocent party, unsuspected.

"Wiz, please take me to see ...

"At that point, the robot began to smoke, falling to the floor and rolling about.

"She was dead."

Abruptly, Hera-Juno-1 started to laugh, almost maniacally.

"What is that noise you are making? I don't understand. Are you sad? Is that crying?" said Wiz.

"No, no. It's laughing. Laughing at what just hit me. It came out of the blue"

"Oh, laughing. I understand. And, this laughing is blue?"

"Just a saying that an idea came from nowhere, out of the blue sky."

"Yes, I now see. What caused this laughing?"

"It was something in a science-fiction book I had read, long ago."

"Science is not fiction. Smart would be upset to hear you say that."

"No, it's a form of story-telling, where speculation is used to tell fictional science stories, bringing imagination into play to make an interesting book or movie."

"Now I understand. So much to learn about your people."

"And, we about the M'Jell," said Hera-Juno-1.

"There is a book, made into a movie, written by Arthur C. Clarke, *2001: A Space Odyssey.*

"In the story there is an intelligent on-board computer, HAL 9000, which went berserk, killing one man and almost killing another, as well as killing three men in hibernation.

"This may be the answer to the murders."

"What do we do next?" said Wiz.

"Not we, you. I'll tell you what to do," said Hera-Juno.

"I'm staying here."

CHAPTER TWENTY-TWO

Deactivation

Upon returning to the M'Jell craft, Wiz met with Smart, Caress, and emergency members of the crew to discuss the implementation of Hera-Juno's plan.

He gave the orders:

"Manually lock operation of the airlock and connected chambers, as well as the doors to all of the craft's rooms, so that they cannot be opened or closed, other than manually.

"Shift propulsion controls to manual.

"Place the power plant operation on standby, maintaining critical internal power with battery backups.

"Order all crew to wear spacesuits at all times.

"Manually close all water and air controls, as well as electrical power.

"We will then go into total shutdown of the craft. Nothing should be operational. The craft must be dead."

***

Smart entered a small, lead-shielded compartment toward the rear, where the craft's AI was housed.

"Quickly," said Wiz. "Disconnect it from all input/output data lines. We need to move fast. It may sense something wrong and try to communicate outside its system. We don't know what it might be capable of doing."

"Done," said Smart. "It's isolated."

"Get your technical staff in here. Have them look at the memory units of the AI, comparing their operations programs with the backup operations programs stored separately. Again, be careful. We don't know what it is capable of, even isolated."

***

"The programs did not match," said Smart. "That of the AI has an additional component, small programs oriented toward following crew members around in certain areas of the craft. Three of the areas match those where the murders took place. Additionally, there are several others, ones where murders were not committed but must have been planned."

"Can your staff clean out the murder programs?" said wiz.

"Possibly, but the best thing would be to wipe all of the AI's programs."

"That might help us," said Wiz. "But it would not help our world. Get your staff to develop a program, a virus, to go into the AI and remove the murder programs.

"I don't understand. Why not just wipe this one, and install the backup program?"

Wiz took a deep breath, relieved, "If we can develop a program to remove the murder program, we can send it to the AI experts in our world, where they can introduce it into the AI systems used in our world by whoever is killing us."

"It will be done," said Smart.

CHAPTER TWENTY-THREE

Rewards

"She's going to die. We need to help her," said Caress.

"Do we know when the Europa Inspector spacecraft will have to escape from the Europa moon's gravitational pull?" said Smart. "According to Hera-Juno, the flybys are getting closer and closer to the moon.

"Yes, in about one week, Earth-time," said Wiz.

"I have a plan. She helped us; we must help her."

Finding out about NASA's requirement for Hera-Juno to move into the deep gravitational field of Jupiter and die, the M'Jell respond by offering help, as a reward to her for solving the murders.

From a large construction airlock on the surface of the M'Jell spacecraft come three construction/repair spheres similar to the one that carried Hera-Juno-2. Guided by a team supervised by Smart, they rapidly get to work on the Inspector spacecraft.

Hera-Juno's spacecraft home is modified to make it able to last for a long time. The solar panels are removed. Small, nuclear-powered rockets and energy generators are added. Heavy radiation shielding is provided. Additional memory storage is added to Inspector's memory bank, including a highly-shielded, protective shelter for a backup of Hera-Juno, one that would self-activate if she were to die or break down due to excessive radiation. All construction waste is directed toward Jupiter for eventual disposal as it is caught in Jupiter's gravitational force.

***

The M'Jell found Hera-Juno to be so different, unique, and something special. She is not an AI, like the murdering spacecraft computer. She much resembles the respected Second Level M'Jell. They cannot understand why she, as a being, lives alone.

Upon a more thorough, very deep inspection of Hera-Juno's memories, Caress, the most sensitive of the M'Jell finds her memories of Dorian, her long-dead love.

"I have found this. It is part of a conversation with Milo, her friend on Earth, long before she became a memory person. I believe that this will help to make her happy.

Yes. I can't accept complete death. That, and another thing. When you were asking about my past life, I almost mentioned him, but couldn't.

Him? I don't understand.

There was a young man, Dorian. I met him with an Irish dance group. So handsome, tall, and strong. Black curly hair like yours.

We were in love. The future was waiting for us. I was so happy. Then, with no warning, he was taken from me and died in weeks from cancer, a fast one.

I never found someone else, didn't want to find anyone. I have always been so alone and angry that it happened, stolen from me. That's why I hate death. I don't want to die; I refuse to die. I will not die!

***

"Hera-Juno, we are concerned about you," said Caress. "If you are to continue elsewhere now that we have modified your craft, rather than being absorbed by Jupiter, we can help you find happiness. You should not be alone.

"We can build your Dorian from your memories, as an AI. It won't be like a real person, but it will be someone to talk to. Isolation is not good. Emotions should be shared with someone."

Hera-Juno, in her long-ago broken heart recalls Dorian.

"Dorian? So long ago. Is it possible? What would it be like?"

"It wouldn't be physical, but mental," said Wiz.

***

Dorian is "reborn". He was not complete, for the M'Jell did not have access to his memories. However, from the remembered pieces and past emotions of Emily Sue Barker who had become Elizabeth Anne Gurley and, later, Hera-Juno, he was formed.

He is confused as to who he is, where he is, and why he exists. Caress, working with Hera-Juno, forms him into a full person. A beginning love, a recovered love is started.

"Emily Sue, why can't I see you? Why can't I see where I am?" said Dorian.

"Do you feel me, my thoughts? My love for you?" said Emily.

"I feel something. Yes, a warmth. Happiness. Is that you? Where have you been?"

Emily Sue explains how she came to be in the spacecraft's memory, and how he came to be, renewed.

Dorian grows, accepting the fact that he died long ago, but is now alive, not as a man, but as a memory.

Together they plan to leave the Jovian system, to explore.

CHAPTER TWENTY-FOUR

Where to Now?

"What do you want to see, Hera-Juno?" said Wiz. "Or should I call you Emily Sue?"

"Hera-Juno is fine for us. Later I will be Emily Sue.

"I want to see everything. I want to go to the far beyond, to see places and peoples of the universe."

'Hera-Juno, It's much bigger than what you can imagine. You will live a long time, but will eventually be absorbed into it as you and your craft deteriorate. It can't be stopped. We all have an end."

"My life has been good, especially now that Dorian is with me. I know that my little spacecraft does not have the speed to travel as fast or as far as yours, but that doesn't matter," she responded.

"Again, thanks for your help, for honoring us. The Third Level of the M'Jell will always remember you. Go forth with our praise," said Wiz, bowing.

"And, I will remember all of you, forever."

***

Using "maps" prepared for her by the M'Jell, Hera-Juno mentally reaches for the controls of the nuclear-powered rockets.

She laughs.

Oort Cloud, here we come! Hold on, Dorian!

CHAPTER TWENTY-FIVE

Evaluation Completed

The M'Jell completed their evaluation of the people of Earth, deciding that they were not advanced enough to consider being part of the greater universe. Wars, non-acceptance of different peoples and cultures and religions, accumulation of more wealth than needed by a few, such that many suffer, and the placement of other cultures and colors and genders and sexual existences and variations at different levels all fail under the empathic evaluation of the aliens.

Then, their traveling world departs from its location on the other side of the Oort Cloud to another solar system to consider further evaluations.

CHAPTER TWENTY-SIX

Confusion and Panic

Jeffers stands next to Berks and Eddie at NASA/KSC, monitoring the Europa Inspector spacecraft's move toward Jupiter's moon, Ganymede.

NASA made a late decision to dispose of the spacecraft by crashing it on Ganymede due to concerns that there might not be enough rocket propellant to reach Jupiter, considering the many flight-path adjustments needed.

"We are receiving a signal from Inspector. She's doing it," said a teary-eyed Eddie. "I can't believe it. What a tough woman."

Berks stared at the monitor. Taking a choking breath, "Yes, she's slowly pulling away from Europa, heading to Ganymede."

***

"Something's wrong," said Berks. "Eddie, get Jeffers in here, quick."

Arriving on the run, breathless, Jeffers said, "What's going on? You say Inspector didn't hit Ganymede? Where is it? Not Europa? Jupiter? One of the other moons?'

"Not only did it not hit Ganymede, it has moved outward from the Jovian system, probably in the direction of Saturn," said Berks.

"What? Saturn? Is she responding?"

"Not really. Just a brief message before she was to hit Ganymede"

"Let me see it."

NOT LIKELY I WILL KEEP IN TOUCH. YOU GUYS HAVE BEEN GREAT TO WORK WITH. HOPE MY DEPARTURE FROM THE SOLAR SYSTEM DOES NOT CAUSE PROBLEMS. GOODBYE. HERA-JUNO.

"Damn! She's gone, but not dead," said Eddie, a big smile on his face. "Good for her."

EPILOGUE

Rogers Berkshire (Berks) and Edmund Faulke (Eddie) ... They assume that Hera-Juno, rather than sending the Europa Inspector plummeting into the moon Ganymede, has decided to leave the Jovian system and head further out into the Solar system. That's about all that they and Jeffers can tell NASA.

Milo and Rosalie ... One last message from Hera-Juno explains what has happened, including Dorian being with her, and telling them to keep it to themselves.

Milo, Rosalie, and the kids often go up to Ellis Hill to turn the telescope on Saturn, knowing she is heading that way. They named their newborn baby girl, Elizabeth Hera. She likes to point at the dark starry sky, imitating Emily and Kenny.

DARPA ... The robot is confiscated by DARPA agents but doesn't work by itself. It was operable only with the controller that Milo built following Missus Gurley's instructions.

The robot, deemed by the Court as being private property, was returned to Milo and the Mann County Museum, where it is used for demonstrations.

The M'Jell ... Fascinated by the story about the lunatic computer, HAL 9000, they downloaded the entire four-book series from an Earth library, amazed that Dave Bowman's spirit had observed creatures deep down in Europa's ocean.

"I still can't figure out why a computer kept asking for my library card number. Something about checking out," said Wiz. "So, I just had the AI download them."

"I loved *2061: Odyssey Two,"* said Smart. "When Bowman went deep under the ice and found life on Europa. That was great.

"And, those words:

ALL THESE WORLDS ARE YOURS --- EXCEPT EUROPA, ATTEMPT NO LANDINGS THERE."

"Not science-fiction. We also sensed them," said Caress. "Very primitive creatures, waiting for something."

"Are the humans in for a surprise!" said Wiz, trying to make a human laughing sound.

"So cool!"

"You know, science is exciting," said Smart. "However, I'm going to try writing some science-fiction. Do you think our M'Jell would like it?"

"From what I have learned from reading about the Earth people, you need an agent," said Wiz.

"What's an agent?" said Smart.

"No idea."

Following up on the M'Jell's successful insertion of the anti-murder program into their traveling world's AI network, stopping additional murders, the Second Level M'Jell conducted an investigation. It was determined that a group of Second Level M'Jell were trying to conduct a takeover of the government.

First Level M'Jell, as judges, and to warn others, moved the perpetrators down to Third Level M'Jell by reprogramming their minds. They do not recall their previous lives as Second Level M'Jell.

The small burnt spherical robot stands on a pedestal in a park in one of the major cities of the M'Jell traveling world. Her name is quietly spoken with reverence by all passing, bowing their heads.

Hera-Juno (Emily Sue Barker or Elizabeth Anne Gurley) ... She's out there, somewhere, moving toward the Oort Cloud.

However, she is no longer alone. Dorian is with her.

APPENDIX

Europa Inspector**

Hera-Juno further prepared herself for her trip as a "stowaway" in the memory storage banks of the Europa Inspector spacecraft by learning as much as she could about the strategy of the project, the power and propulsion of the spacecraft, and the rocket, the launch and trajectory of the spacecraft, and, most important, the scientific package. This latter was most important, as she was likely to become involved in its operation.

The goals of the Europa Inspector spacecraft are to explore the moon Europa, investigate its potential for or presence of life, and aid in the selection of a landing site for the future **Europa Lander**. This exploration is focused on understanding the three main requirements for life: liquid water, chemistry, and energy. Specifically, the objectives are to study:

Ice shell and ocean: Confirm the existence, and characterize the nature, of water within or beneath the ice, and processes of surface-ice-ocean exchange

Composition: Distribution and chemistry of key compounds and the links to ocean composition

Geology: Characteristics and formation of surface features, including sites of recent or current activity.

STRATEGY

Because Europa lies well within the harsh radiation fields surrounding Jupiter, even a radiation-hardened spacecraft in near orbit would be functional for just a few months. Most of the instruments gather data far faster than the communications system can transmit it to Earth because there are a limited number of antennas available on Earth to receive scientific data. Therefore, another key limiting factor in science for a Europa orbiter is the time available to return data to Earth. In contrast, the amount of time during which the instruments can make close-up observations is less important.

Studies by the Jet Propulsion Laboratory show that by performing several flybys with many months to return data, the Europa Inspector will be able to conduct the most crucial measurements. While Inspector orbits Jupiter at a distance to avoid the heavy radiation load, it uses gravity assists from Europa, Ganymede, and Callisto to change the trajectory into a series of elliptical orbits followed by flybys. Between each of the flybys, the spacecraft, then in the outer sweep of their elliptical orbits, will have seven to ten days to transmit data stored during each brief encounter. That will let the spacecraft have up to a year to transmit its data.

The Europa Inspector will not orbit Europa but will orbit Jupiter and conduct forty-five flybys of Europa at altitudes from 25 km to 2,700 km (16 mi to 1,678 mi) each during its 3.5-year mission. A key feature of the mission concept is that the Inspector would use gravity assists from Europa, Ganymede, and Callisto to change its trajectory, allowing the spacecraft to return to a different close approach point with each flyby. Each flyby would cover a different sector of Europa to achieve a medium-quality global topographic survey, including ice thickness. The Europa Inspector will attempt to fly by at low altitude through the plumes of water vapor erupting from the moon's ice crust, thus sampling its subsurface ocean without having to land on the surface and drill through the ice.

The spacecraft is expected to receive a total ionizing dose of 2.8 megarad during the mission. Shielding from Jupiter's harsh radiation belt will be provided by a radiation vault with 0.3 inches (7.6 mm) thick titanium-aluminum alloy walls, which will enclose the spacecraft electronics. To maximize the effectiveness of this shielding, the electronics will also be nested deep in the core of the spacecraft for additional radiation protection.

POWER

Although solar power is only one percent as intense at Jupiter as it is in Earth's orbit, powering a Jupiter orbital spacecraft with solar panels was demonstrated by the earlier Juno mission. The mission's designers determined that solar power was both cheaper than plutonium and practical to use on the spacecraft. Despite the increased weight of solar panels compared to plutonium-powered generators, the vehicle's mass had been projected to still be within acceptable launch limits. Solar panels were chosen to power Europa Inspector.

Initial analysis suggested that each panel will have a surface area of 18 m2 (190 sq ft) and produce 150 watts continuously when pointed towards the Sun while orbiting Jupiter. While in Europa's shadow, batteries will enable the spacecraft to continue gathering data. However, ionizing radiation can damage solar panels. The Europa Inspector's orbit will pass through Jupiter's intense magnetosphere, which is expected to gradually degrade the solar panels as the mission progresses.

PROPULSION

The propulsion subsystem is 3 meters (10 ft) tall, 1.5 meters (5 ft) in diameter, and comprises about two-thirds of the spacecraft's main body. The propulsion subsystem initially carries nearly 2,700 kilograms (6,000 lb) of monomethyl hydrazine and dinitrogen tetroxide propellant, 50 to 60 percent of which will be used for the 6 to 8-hour Jupiter orbit insertion burn. The spacecraft has a total of 24 rocket engines rated at 27.5N (6.2lbf) thrust for attitude control and propulsion. Small iodine-ion thruster units provide for mobility adjustments while orbiting Europa in the flybys.

SCIENTIFIC PAYLOAD

The Europa Inspector mission is equipped with a suite of 9 instruments to study Europa's interior and ocean, geology, chemistry, and habitability. The electronic components will be protected from the intense radiation by a 150-kilogram titanium-aluminum shield. The science instruments for the orbiter are listed below:

The **Europa Thermal Emission Imaging System (E-THEMIS)** will provide high spatial resolution as well as multi-spectral imaging of the surface of Europa in the mid to far-infrared bands to help detect geologically active sites and areas, such as potential vents erupting plumes of water into space.

The **Mapping Imaging Spectrometer for Europa (MISE)** is an imaging near-infrared spectrometer to probe the surface composition of Europa, identifying and mapping the distributions of organics (including amino acids and tholins, salts, acid hydrates, water-ice phases, and other materials. From these measurements, scientists expect to be able to relate the moon's surface composition to the habitability of its ocean.

The **Europa Imaging System (EIS)** is a visible spectrum imaging suite consisting of two cameras to map Europa's surface and study smaller areas in high resolution, as low as 0.5 m (20 in) per pixel.

The **Wide-angle Camera (WAC)** has a field of view of 48° by 24° and a resolution of 11 m (36 ft) from a 50 km (31 mi) altitude. The WAC will obtain stereo-imagery swaths throughout the mission.

The **Narrow-angle Camera (NAC)** has a 2.3° by 1.2° field of view, giving it a resolution of 0.5 m (20 in) per pixel from a 50 km (31 mi) altitude. The NAC is mounted on a 2-axis gimbal, allowing it to point at specific targets regardless of the main spacecraft's orientation. This will allow for mapping of >95% of Europa's surface at a resolution of ≤50 m (160 ft) per pixel. For reference, only around 14% of Europa's surface has previously been mapped at a resolution of ≤500 m (1,600 ft) per pixel.

The **Europa Ultraviolet Spectrograph (Europa-UVS)**instrument will be able to detect small plumes and will provide valuable data about the composition and dynamics of the moon's exosphere.

The **Radar for Europa Assessment and Sounding: Ocean to Near-surface (REASON)** is a dual-frequency ice-penetrating radar instrument that is designed to characterize and sound Europa's ice crust from the near-surface to the ocean, revealing the hidden structure of Europa's ice shell and potential water pockets within.

The **Europa Inspector Magnetometer (EIM)** will be used to characterize the magnetic fields around Europa. The instrument consists of three magnetic flux-gates placed along a 25 ft boom, which will be stowed during launch and deployed afterward. By studying the strength and orientation of Europa's magnetic field over multiple flybys, scientists hope to be able to confirm the existence of Europa's subsurface ocean, as well as characterize the thickness of its icy crust and measure the water's depth and salinity.

The **Plasma Instrument for Magnetic Sounding (PIMS)** measures the plasma surrounding Europa to characterize the magnetic fields generated by plasma currents. These plasma currents mask the magnetic induction response of Europa's subsurface ocean. In conjunction with a magnetometer, it is key to determining Europa's ice shell thickness, ocean depth, and salinity. PIMS will also probe the mechanisms responsible for weathering and releasing material from Europa's surface into the atmosphere and ionosphere and understand how Europa influences its local space environment and Jupiter's magnetosphere.

The **Mass Spectrometer for Planetary Exploration (MASPEX)** will determine the composition of the surface and subsurface ocean by measuring Europa's extremely tenuous atmosphere and any surface materials ejected into space.

The **Surface Dust Analyzer (SUDA))** is a mass spectrometer that will measure the composition of small solid particles ejected from Europa, providing the opportunity to directly sample the surface and potential plumes on low-altitude flybys. The instrument is capable of identifying traces of organic and inorganic compounds in the ice of ejecta. Scientists expect SUDA to be able to detect a single cell in an ice grain.

Additionally:

Gravity/Radio Science.

While not intended for use specifically as an instrument, Inspector will be using its high-gain radio antenna to perform additional experiments and learn about Europa's gravitational field. As the spacecraft performs each of its forty-five flybys, its trajectory will be subtly altered by the moon's gravity. By sending radio signals between Earth and the moon and characterizing the Doppler shift in the return signal, scientists will be able to create a detailed characterization of the spacecraft's motion. This data will help to determine how Europa flexes with its distance from Jupiter, which will in turn reveal information about the moon's internal structure and tidal motions.

LAUNCH AND TRAJECTORY

The ~840 m/s (1,900 mph) delta-V Jupiter orbit insertion burn will take place at a distance of 11 Rj (Jovian radii) from the planet following a 500 km (310 mi) Ganymede gravity assist flyby to reduce spacecraft velocity by ~400 m/s (890 mph). After this, the spacecraft will perform a ~122 m/s (270 mph) periapsis raise maneuver (PRM) rocket burn near the apoapsis of its initial 202-day period capture orbit.

It was announced that the mission would use a 5.5-year trajectory to the Jovian system, with gravity-assist maneuvers involving Mars and Earth.

The Falcon Heavy was chosen to launch the spacecraft.

** Extracted/modified by Missus Gurley in partial form from **Wikipedia.**

John Charles Miller (floridamiller@verizon.net) is a groundwater geologist and a writer of speculative fiction, bizarre short stories, and poetry since 2005. He resides in Tampa, Florida with his wife Mary. They have a small cabin on Lake Tsala Apopka near the community of Hernando in Citrus County, Florida.

Citrus County and its wonderful people often drive the storylines of his novels.

He is a member of the Citrus Writers of Florida Group.

During forty years as a geologist, he focused on groundwater supplies and contamination assessments, monitoring, and cleanup. Retired, he has held Professional Geologist (PG) licenses in California, Delaware, Florida, and Indiana.

He is fluent in Spanish, having served in the US Peace Corps in the Dominican Republic from 1962-64 under John F. Kennedy's presidency He has eight years of professional hydrogeological experience in Latin America, having worked in Argentina, The Dominican Republic, Mexico, Panama, Peru, and Puerto Rico.

In 2023, he and Landy Orozco-Uribe of Morelia, Mexico, published a dual-language (English/Spanish) collection of John's short stories and novelettes, *Wheels & Ruedas*.

His stories have been award winners in annual contests of the Tampa Writers Alliance (TWA) and the Florida Writers Association (FWA). His short story, *Scammed*, took 1st Place in the Science Fiction/Fantasy category in the 2009 TWA annual writing contest. *Las Ruedas* (2012), *Taking the Bait* (2015), and *Words from the Earth* (2020*)*, all short stories, and a poem *Morning Walk* (2014*)*, were FWA Annual Collection award winners.

A list of his writings is included at the beginning of this book. All are available from Amazon.com as eBooks or paperbacks, or from the author (floridamiller@verizon.net).

Made in the USA
Columbia, SC
30 October 2024

45087408R00070